A PLACE CALLED
NUNNERY

A PLACE CALLED NUNNERY

INGE BLANTON

iUniverse LLC
Bloomington

A PLACE CALLED NUNNERY

iUniverse books may be ordered through booksellers or by contacting:

iUniverse LLC
1663 Liberty Drive
Bloomington, IN 47403
www.iuniverse.com
1-800-Authors (1-800-288-4677)

ISBN: 978-1-4917-0321-2 (sc)
ISBN: 978-1-4917-0322-9 (ebk)

Printed in the United States of America

iUniverse rev. date: 08/20/2013

A place called Nunnery. This story is not about Nuns, but about Naomi Atossa; about her survival and courage in the face of almost overwhelming adversity.

Other stories by Inge Blanton are:

Lost in Time.
The story of a young woman swept up by a time-warp. She is thrown so far back in time she can find no landmarks she can identify. But she meets fascinating people and has many interesting adventures.

The Antarean Odyssey
The Antarean Odyssey is the birth of a people and the fiery end of their homeworld. It covers eight books.

The Labors of Jonathan; Book ONE
One night Jonathan overhears about a world wide cartel, and interstellar trade agreement and aliens named Altruscans.

The Original Four; Book Two
Sabrina, Sarah, Ayhlean and Kamila, four orphans are the beginning of the Antarean people.

Loss of Eden; Book Three

The ending of childhood might feel like the loss of Eden. It is time for The Four to meet the world.

Starship Trefayne; Book Four

If Sargon aka Jim Thalon thought to have Sabrina safely on the Trefayne, he will soon learn otherwise.

Misalliance; Book Five

To fulfill the Planetary Alliance requirement, Commander Sarah Thalon, chief medical officer of the Antares becomes an intern on the planet Madras

Assignment Earth; Book Six.

Sabrina's assignment is to see if Earth is ready to join the Planetary Alliance.

Matched: Book Seven.

Sabrina finally finds a mate who is her match in almost everything.

I, Sargon; Book Eight.

This is the life history of Sargon, aka Jim Thalon.

A book in the making is Bortei,

Queen of Atlan

"My name is Alma, it's the name my mother gave me, and it's been good enough for me."

"Accept the name Bortei."

Chapter One

Class was over. Everybody filed out of the auditorium, except for Naomi. She sat in her seat, oblivious of the shuffling feet and murmuring voices. Her whole mind was focused inward on what to decide, civil law or interstellar law. The way she felt right now, she didn't care to decide on anything. With a deep mental sigh, she thought, what does it matter? Caleb is dead.

Caleb's death would not go away. They had been inseparable, had grown up together. Later, they had studied law and in time would have married. Now there was this unbearable void. Going on alone was difficult. She still felt the guilt . . . she had survived the car crash; he had died.

Now if I go into civil law, she though, I would have only two more semesters. But then what? Stay on Sarpedion, or go home to Novalis? Thinking of Novalis she shuddered; too many bad memories. If I go with interstellar law, I could become an ambassador like Aunt Mariam. I wouldn't have to settle anywhere in particular. Unconsciously, Naomi made a face. One path would take her far afield, but with the other, she could finish sooner. She sighed. There wasn't the incentive of staying in school anymore. I guess I'll take civil law and finish sooner, she finally decided. Suddenly, she heard a gurgling sound and wondered where it was coming from.

"Hungry?"

Naomi turned and looked up into the amused face of a girl standing next to her seat. Embarrassed, she realized the sound had come from her stomach. Naomi blushed. "Sorry, I haven't had breakfast." Checking her watch, she exclaimed, "Good gracious. Long winded, wasn't he?"

The girl grinned, and stepped across Naomi's feet.

Gathering her books, Naomi rose and noticed the auditorium had nearly emptied. From the Law Center, she walked to the cafeteria, only to find that it was full. Of course it's full, she groused. Her class should have ended over half an hour ago. The professor was good. She had to give him that, but he was not well liked. He gave too many pop quizzes and didn't know when to quit.

Today's menu was sliced roast beef. Not bad, Naomi thought, and ordered it on a bun with fries and a drink. Carrying the tray, she searched for an empty seat and spotted a table by a window someone was just vacating. She quickly made her way to claim it and was in the process of moving her food from the tray to the table when a male voice asked, "Mind if I join you?"

Naomi looked up at the voice's owner. He was of medium build, with a dark complexion, thick, dark hair and dark eyes and was smiling at her.

"No, of course not," Naomi said, as she sat down. She had just taken the first bite out of her bun when he asked if she was a student. Not too pleased with his timing, she quickly swallowed the whole thing, then, answered, "Yes."

"Do you live in Vasilika or on campus?"

"My parents live in Vasilika; I live on campus."

There was a lengthy pause while they both ate. Then he asked, "What are you studying?"

"Law."

"Heavy subject?" he asked, raising his eyebrows.

"No not really. But soon, I have to decide if I want to go into interstellar law or stay with civil law."

"Well, you need to decide then what would best serve you for your future."

"That's easier said than done. Are you student or faculty?"

"I'm sort of faculty. I'm employed in an advisory capacity. Sorry, I didn't introduce myself. My name is Eddan el Halugh. And your name is?"

"Naomi Atossa."

"You're not from Sarpedion?"

"No, Novalis."

"Oh the Omicron V System. You're planets away from home."

"My mother is faculty, and my father is attached to our embassy's law department."

"And your mother?"

"She teaches astronomy."

"I see."

Sipping her drink, she thought for a moment, then, it clicked. "You're from the planet Madras, aren't you?"

"Yes, but I have a permanent residence on Sarpedion."

"What's your advisory capacity?"

"I counsel off-world students when they first arrive here."

Finishing the last of her drink, she rose and picked up her tray to dispose of the trash. "It was nice chatting with you," she said politely.

She walked out of the cafeteria and grimaced. He's a bit to nosey, she thought and gave it a mental shrug. Two days later she saw him again. She was having lunch on a bench, enjoying the warm sun when he walked up.

"Hello, Naomi Atossa. How nice to see you again," he said and sat down beside her.

"Hello, Mister el Halugh," Naomi replied.

"Please, call me Eddan."

"On your lunch break?"

"Sort of. You still have a class?"

"Yes, a two-hour one."

"Do you know there's going to be a concert on the South Oval, at five? Would you like to join me?"

"I don't know, I . . ."

"I have two tickets," he interjected, quickly. "Maybe afterwards, we could grab a bite to eat."

Naomi looked at him. *Pushy guy,* she thought and was about to rise when he made another appeal, "Please. I hate to waste a good ticket."

Naomi, pursing her lips, considered him for a second, then, shrugged. "All right, meet me about four-twenty at the law center."

* * * *

Naomi exited the law center a little after four-twenty and caught sight of Eddan at the bottom of the steps. As she descended, she noticed he was well dressed, and just a little closer, his cologne wafted her way. She didn't mind men wearing scent, as long as it was discrete. His was a bit too obvious.

"I'm glad you agreed to join me, Naomi. It's so much nicer when you can share an experience, and the performance should be a good one," he said as he fell in beside her.

"Thank you for inviting me," Naomi responded, formally.

The concert was held outdoors at the large, partially sunken garden theater on the South Oval, and Naomi enjoyed it more than she had expected. Afterwards, their dinner date came off just as nice. She was usually shy around strangers so was pleased that he carried the conversation. Most of his comments covered the unusual events foreign students experience being new to Sarpedion. He said very little about himself. After dinner, she thanked him for the pleasant evening. When he tried to take her home, she turned down his offer, explaining she'd rather walk home by herself.

All during the semester she continued to catch sight of him. He was at the swimming pool, at a garden party given by the Embassy, in the cafeteria, or passing her on her way home. Naomi was becoming more and more disconcerted by the persistent attention. She didn't know what to make of him, or why he had so obviously attached himself to her. Uncomfortable by his pursuit, she made a point to offer him no encouragement by being casual in her responses, and by declining most of his invitations, but all her efforts failed to dissuade him.

At her wits' end, she decided to speak to her parents about it.

* * * *

Naomi lived on campus to allow her parents more elbow room. The Embassy had provided an apartment for them, but it was somewhat crowded when she stayed there. Besides, she was twenty-five and it was gently intimated it was time for her to be on her own.

When she arrived at her parents' apartment complex, Neila Raban, the next door neighbor, rushed agitatedly down the stairs to meet her. "Naomi, my dear," she panted, "I'm sorry, but your mother has had a heart attack and she's at the hospital."

Naomi stared at her, mute, so Neila repeated her message.

Naomi's insides froze and she felt as if all life had drained from her. She covered her face with both hands thinking, no, not Mother. She could not bear losing anyone else.

The neighbor tugged at her sleeve. "Would you like for me to drive you?"

Naomi lifted her head. "No. No thank you. I'll call a taxi."

"You can use my phone."

Naomi went inside to make the call, but waited on the steps for the taxi. She was never at ease with strangers. She knew Mrs. Raban's hovering was just her nature. Sympathy and friendliness oozed from her every comment and gesture. Naomi shuddered at the intrusiveness of it. She was glad when the taxi pulled up.

When she arrived at the hospital, her father was standing at a window outside the intensive care unit. His hunched shoulders made him appear small and forlorn.

"Father?"

He slowly turned toward her. "Naomi," he said and held out his hands to her.

She looked at him, noticing his face was strained and tired. She put her hands into his. "What happened?" she asked.

He brushed a shaky hand across his forehead. "We were going out for the evening and needed to leave, but she was still in her dressing room. I became worried that she was taking so long, so I went to check and found her lying unconscious on the floor. I followed the ambulance here and still have yet to be told anything."

"Neila Raban said she had a heart attack."

"I don't know. I just told her that. It was the first thing that came to my mind."

Naomi tugged at his hand. "Why don't you sit down and I'll see if I can get some information from one of the nurses." Naomi waited until he was seated before she went to the nurse's station. After identifying herself, she asked what was happening.

"As far as I know, they're still running tests."

"Did she have a heart attack?"

"No, we don't think so. She probably just fainted."

"Will you tell me when you find out? My father is very distraught."

The nurse glanced in her father's direction and then back at her. "I can very well imagine. As soon as I see the doctor, I'll ask."

"Thank you." Naomi went back to her father and sat down beside him to wait. It took another half hour before a man in a white coat strode purposefully toward them.

Naomi jumped up and walked swiftly to meet him. Looking at his tag, she addressed him, "Doctor Sardo, I'm Naomi Atossa. How is my mother?"

"Miss Atossa, we have run several tests, which indicate she is anemic and has some type of blood disorder. I have ordered further tests."

Naomi's father had joined them and was standing beside his daughter. "When can I see her?" he asked, his voice husky.

"In about twenty minutes. We're still trying to stabilize her. I'm sorry I can't give you better news."

"Thank you, Doctor," Naomi said

Anxiously, Naomi's eyes followed her father as he listlessly shuffled back to the bench they had been sitting on. Naomi sat down next to him, putting her hand through his arm. "Father?"

"I'm all right, Naomi," he said, patting her hand. "I'm just very worried. I fear this won't be something simple that'll just go away. But, we'll deal with it."

Twenty minutes later a nurse came. "Mister Atossa, you can see your wife now."

He only looked at the nurse. It didn't register that he had been addressed by his wife's name. As they walked into her room, Lia was lying still, her face pale against the pillow. Her eyes were closed and she looked diminished under the covers.

Like Naomi, she was petite, with the same auburn hair and dark hazel eyes. Only the nose and mouth were different. Naomi's lips were fuller, and her nose lacked the little hump on its ridge.

Jarrod walked up to the bed and gently took her hand. With his voice barely audible, he said, "Lia?"

"Jarrod," she whispered. "I'm so sorry."

"Lia my love." His hand brushed back a strand of her hair as he cautiously sat on the edge of her bed.

"Mother?" Naomi said, but Lia had sunk back into unconsciousness.

Naomi's eyes teared. She had never seen her mother helpless. It was Lia who had always been the strong one. Her father was a gentle man, sometimes detached in manner.

After a while her father spoke, "Naomi, you still have to go to school. You will miss your class if you don't go now."

"But . . ."

"I will stay with your mother."

* * * *

A week later, Lia was released from the hospital. As soon as Naomi heard, she went to their home. The maid informed her that her mother was in her bedroom.

The door was ajar, but Naomi knocked before sticking her head into the room.

"May I come in?"

"Yes, Love, of course."

"What are you doing?"

Her mother sat on her bed which was strewn with papers she was sorting. She put down the sheaves she was holding to look at her daughter who stood frowning. "Naomi, I will have to go home . . ."

"Not the Nunnery!" Naomi exclaimed. "You hated it there."

Lia gazed into Naomi's face, and there was a struggle in her not to soften. "Now daughter . . ." then, she gave her a searching look, "Your father hasn't said anything, yet?"

"I haven't seen him."

Lia's chest rose in a heavy sigh. "Naomi, what the hospital found is that I have blood disorder, and there is no cure for it. It is degenerative."

"You have a blood disorder?"

Lia continued, ignoring the interruption. "Your father and I have decided to go back to Novalis. You will stay here and get your degree. Then, you can make up your mind whether to stay or come home."

"Naturally, this was all decided without consulting me," Naomi retorted, acidly. "Did it ever occur to you that I would like to be with you? Maybe take care of you . . . They said there's no cure?"

"No. There is none. Little anyone can do about it. Naomi dear, don't be so upset; I am deciding about my life, and you are free to choose. My advice to you is to stay here and finish school."

"Oh, Mom, I still don't know which way I want to go."

"What I wish for you is to finish this time, and not to change your major again. You can't always start anew. Finish this time."

Naomi teared up. "But I will be here all alone and worry myself sick about you," she protested.

"I will be fine, and so will you," Lia said soothingly. Her hand stroked Naomi's cheek. "It's only two more semesters if you take civil law, and then you can come home."

"But the Nunnery?"

The Nunnery used to be just that, a convent. Seven hundred years ago it had been an endowment from a king to Lia's family. One of Lia's ancestors, an abbess, had converted it into the convent, and the nuns had taken care of impoverished widows and girls in trouble. After about five hundred years, the order was disbanded. The house, lands and a small village were returned to the Atossa family. The last abbess, also an ancestress of the Atossa family, set up a charter and mandated that the property would pass from mother to daughter, not from father to son, as was customary. So it had been for the last two hundred years. The Nunnery became a refuge, a place to return home. It was predominately inhabited by older women and men, and sometimes penniless widows with young children.

Lia had left the Nunnery, when Sarah, Lia's mother, would not accept Jarrod Darbani as Lia's husband. There was also a long-standing grievance between the two families resulting from an illegal maneuver by one of the Darbanis against a member of the Atossa family which had yet to be redressed, or forgiven. Lia married Jarrod despite the objection, and a rift developed between mother and daughter. So Lia left, but now, ill, with her life-expectancy diminishing, she decided to return home.

Chapter Two

Naomi sat in the cafeteria staring despondently at nothing. Yesterday morning, her parents had left for Novalis. Being alone for the first time in her life was a novel experience and frightening. There was an immense stellar space between her parents' world and the one on which she was living.

"Hello, Naomi. I haven't seen you for some time," said a soothing male voice, interrupting her thoughts.

"Oh Eddan," she responded, forgetting for the first time to call him Mister Halugh. She began to cry and he put his arm consolingly around her shoulder.

"What happened?"

"My parents left. My mother is very ill and wished to go back home to Novalis. She basically ordered me to stay and finish my studies," Naomi explained, aggrieved.

"But in the long run this will turn out to be a very wise decision on her part." He paused there, then his comforting voice continued, "If you allow me, I'll help you." Eddan pulled out a chair and sat down, then, solicitously began patting her hand.

"Yesterday, I switched from interstellar to civil law. It will take less time to graduate."

"You're homesick for Novalis?"

"Yes, I want to go home, but, worse, I wish my parents hadn't left."

"I can well imagine how you will miss them."

"Do you miss Madras?"

"No. I like living on Sarpedion. I have no desire to go back to Madras."

"Don't you miss your family?"

"No. I have been gone a long time. This evening, why don't you let me take you out to dinner?"

She took a deep breath. "I really have to study," she replied and exhaled slowly, hoping he would take the hint. She didn't know whether she could cope with Eddan el Halugh.

"But it will do you good to get out. At least for a little while," he insisted, and she agreed.

For the next few months, Eddan began coming around more often. Several times he arrived uninvited to her dorm. At first, his attentions were low-key, but later became more persistent. He began asking her out, escorting her home, and making certain she ate. Soon, Eddan became her sole companion. He was a good conversationalist, talking about the gossip on campus, the theater, and books they both were interested in. He began to help her with her studies, giving her encouragement and confidence.

One day, just before the end of the semester, Eddan came to her dorm with a bunch of roses and asked, "When are we getting married?"

Taking the flowers, Naomi only smiled at him. She hoped he was joking.

* * * *

Naomi sat in her overstuffed easy chair, a law book in her lap, nibbling a cookie when Eddan walked in. She looked up as the door opened and Eddan strode in without knocking with one hand in his pocket and an irate expression on his face. "I haven't heard from you. It would be nice if you'd call once in a while instead of leaving me guessing at what's going on."

Naomi bit her tongue to refrain from telling him what she thought; instead she calmly explained, "Eddan, it's close to finals. I have to study."

"I know, I know. It's just that I miss you."

She gazed at him, silently, keeping her smile polite.

He stepped quickly to her chair, squatting down close, with a hand resting on her knee. "Naomi, you know I have been thinking that we are really getting along well. I have fallen in love with you. I think you and I could be a family. Both of us are alone. Being together, we would be good for each other. Don't do you think?"

"Eddan, I don't know . . ."

He rose and bending forward, moved a strand of hair behind her ear. "Naomi, you don't have to decide this minute, or today, but I want you to think about it," he said, aiming a wistful smile at her. Then, for the first time he kissed her gently on the mouth. Naomi almost recoiled and hoped he hadn't noticed. He continued, "I bet you're hungry. I'm going to get us something to eat while you finish what you're studying."

After the door closed behind him, Naomi sat very still. Why didn't I tell him that I have not intention of ever marrying? Or at least not for a long time. Oh Caleb, why did you die? Why was I left alive and have to live without you? She gazed at the door and shuddered. There is no way I can picture myself married to Eddan. She winced. Putting the thought from her mind, she went back to her book and fairly forgot about Eddan. Two hours later, her stomach demanded her attention and she looked at the clock. Wonder where he went? Well if he doesn't come soon I'll go and get something to eat myself. She shut down her laptop and was in the process of putting her book away, when he came through the door.

"I almost gave up on you," she told him.

"I'm sorry," he said, and smiled. "I brought some cuisine from Madras. I hope you like it."

He didn't mention his proposal all evening. When he left, he only patted her cheek and closed the door softly behind him.

Naomi sat in her chair and chewed at her thumbnail. I whish I could talk to someone. Her feelings about Eddan were ambiguous. He seemed to be around, but that was all one could say about him. If only he would leave me alone, but he was persistent. Nothing she did or said deterred him. And as he said, they were both alone. In the past, she had at least a few acquaintances, but now they seemed to have faded away. She had no real friends since coming to Sarpedion. She sorely missed her mother.

I wonder how she is. I should have had mail by now.

* * * *

Finals were over and she had earned a 4-point. Now, she had only one more semester to go and no one with whom to share her elation, except for Eddan, so she called to tell him.

"Congratulations," he said, his voice affable enough, though not excited. "I always knew you would do well." Then he continued in a careless, good-humoring manner, "Naomi, guess what? I booked a cruise for us. The ship's name is Dream Boat. Can you imagine a name like that for a ship? We will be leaving in two days."

"What . . . !"

"Naomi, it will be good for you to get out of Vasilika and away from campus," he cajoled.

"But Eddan!" Naomi protested. "I'm going home, home to Novalis to see about my mother."

"Your mother is probably fine, otherwise they would have written by now."

"But . . ."

"Naomi, you don't understand. Think of this as a chance of a lifetime," he wheedled. "It was a special offer and I didn't want to let it slip through our fingers. Just think; half price! I thought the two of us could use a vacation. Say yes."

There was a sigh and a slight pause. "How long will this cruise last?"

"Only one week."

Knowing him, she knew he would keep at her until she gave in. Then one week, ten days, won't be too long to spend with him. He was okay for a short spurt, but then I'll leave for Novalis. After the cruise,

I would have to stay in Vasilika twelve more days. Anyway, the cruise will shorten the waiting, Naomi rationalized.

"All right, I'll go."

"You'll have to pack today. We need to leave tomorrow morning. I thought we'd take a train ride to the coast, to Parma, the ship's home port. Won't that be great?"

Naomi considered it. She had never ridden in a train, but had always wanted to.

"I will pick you up about seven in the morning," he broke into her thoughts. "We need to be at the train station at least by eight."

"I'll be ready."

She hung up, changed her clothes, and headed to the Embassy of Novalis. She couldn't understand why she had no news of her mother and it worried her.

She was received by the Ambassador personally, but only because he was familiar with the name Atossa. Her mother's sister was an interstellar ambassador.

"Naomi, I don't understand this either," he said after she explained her concerns. "You should have had news by now."

"That's why I think I should go home.

"When do you think you will want to leave here?"

"There's a spaceship leaving in twenty days for Novalis. I have already made a reservation. In the meantime, I was invited to accompany a friend on a cruise. It's only for one week. So, the moment I return, I will contact you. The cruise ship is the Dream Boat. Its home-port is in Parma. I will be traveling with a man named Eddan el Halugh from Madras. As soon as I return, I'm going home. I brought all the necessary papers with me. Would you be so kind as to have them processed?"

"Leave everything to me and enjoy your trip. I will have everything in order when you come back."

"You are very kind. Thank you so much. I greatly appreciate your assistance, and I will absolutely contact you immediately upon my return."

Chapter Three

For once, Eddan was punctual. He arrived at her dorm by seven with a taxi and helped load her suitcases. By seven-thirty, they were at the train station.

"We're early," Naomi said, looking at her watch.

"We can always have breakfast, then, browse around for something to read on the train."

"Not a bad idea," Naomi agreed. Reading was better than having to listen to Eddan talk.

They had just come up from the underground concourse when Naomi stopped. The noise was incredible as the train roared into the station and slid to a halt, the doors flying open and people spilling out.

"Let's wait until the crowd has thinned, then we'll look for our compartment," Eddan suggested. "It's number fourteen."

Everyone hurried past them. Some had trouble getting porters. There were cries of joy at seeing loved ones. Because it was her first time at a train station, Naomi was somewhat overwhelmed by the bustle and noise of people and machines. There were no trains on Novalis.

After a while, Eddan nudged her and said, "Let's go and find our compartment." They walked slowly alongside the train, scanning for the number. "There it is," Eddan called out.

The compartment was empty and Naomi wondered if it was one of Eddan's contrivances. After getting comfortably settled by the window with Eddan on the opposite seat, Naomi was startled by a sudden shrill whistle. The train jerked, then, slowly at first, but soon picked up speed. It didn't take long before the station was far behind and Naomi began to watch the country scenery fly passed. To her surprise, the train slowed. Probably responding to a signal, Naomi thought. For some time the train crawled along while another one, going in the opposite direction, sped past them. Then another train came alongside, and for a while ran parallel. As Naomi and Eddan watched the compartments sliding by, they glimpsed a couple in an ardent embrace. They looked at each other and began to laugh.

As soon as Vasilika was behind them, Eddan seemed to relax. His mood lightened and he became talkative and funny at times. He presented the whole trip to her as an adventure into the unknown. Amused, Naomi entered into the spirit of it. At noon, a porter knocked on their door, telling them that the dining car was open."

"Hungry yet?" Eddan asked.

"Not so much hungry as stiff. Let's see what the menu offers, then I'll tell you whether I'm hungry," Naomi teased.

When they entered the diner, there was a small table set for two by a window. "Did you arrange this?" Naomi asked.

"Naomi this is a magical journey into the unknown. We don't ask questions." He looked at her with a curious smile paired with a glint in his eyes.

After dinner and back in their compartment, they settled in and for a while read the books they had purchased. Sometime, during the afternoon, Naomi had fallen asleep over her book. Eddan's shuffling a deck of cards startled her awake.

"Want to play?" he asked when she looked sleepily at him, with only one eye open.

"Your book's not interesting enough?" Naomi teased him.

"It is, but now I'd like to do something different."

"When's supper?"

"In about an hour."

She gave him a surprised look. "I'm sorry. Did I sleep all this time?"

Eddan only smiled in response.

As night came, making ready for bed, Naomi and Eddan pulled pillows and blankets down from an overhead storage. During the night, Naomi awakened several times, wondering whether Eddan felt as uncomfortable as she about sleeping in such close proximity, or if he was sleeping as deeply as he seemed to be. He lay very still, and as she listened, there was no sound of his breathing. Maybe it's drowned out by the noise of the train. At least, he's not snoring.

* * * *

The next morning when Naomi woke up, she saw Eddan sitting in the opposite seat. She tensed and blushed slightly, realizing that he had been watching her.

He was already fully dressed with every hair in place as if he hadn't slept at all. When he looked at her, she noticed that only his mouth smiled while his eyes remained expressionless. "Did you sleep well?" he asked.

"Surprisingly well," Naomi told him as she shook the wrinkles out of her dress and stretched. "What's on our agenda for today?"

"We will reach the seaport in about three hours. That will make it around ten o'clock. Then we have half an hour to board our ship. So, after freshening up, the dining car and breakfast should be on our agenda."

"You seem to have everything arranged," Naomi remarked, dryly.

"I always try to be prepared," Eddan told her, smiling. The smile was bland. She couldn't decide if he was pleased with himself, or just simply stating a fact.

On their way to the diner, Naomi wondered why she had let herself be talked into coming with him, especially after he proposed. I hope he doesn't consider this a getting to know each other trip. Before leaving, she had told him that as soon as they were back in Vasilika, she was going to Novalis. But what she didn't tell him was that she had already been in contact with Novalis' ambassador and given him her papers. Eddan had ignored her comment as if he hadn't heard it.

During their time on the train, so far, Eddan's behavior was very proper. He had kissed her only the one time, and since then had made no attempts at being familiar. But still, in the back of her mind, something nagged at her, something that was not quite right.

When they arrived at Parma, Naomi felt hustled off the train, into a cab, and onto the ship, with no time to get her bearing. On board, they had adjacent cabins with a connecting door.

Naomi was barely settled, when the ship departed. In the meantime, she took a shower and unpacked her suitcases. She had just finished dressing when there was a knock on the connecting door, and Eddan came through it.

"The gong for lunch should sound in a few minutes," he told her. "Lunch is buffet style, so we need not hurry. How do you like our trip so far?"

"I don't know yet, Eddan. All we seem to be doing is rushing around."

"Ah, but soon it will slow down and you can rest. Tomorrow, we will arrive at the bay and for the day, our agenda will be sightseeing. There's a ruin on a promontory, a very old castle, and on our second stop, we'll visit a temple." Just then the promised gong announced the meal, and with a flourish Eddan opened the door for her.

Since the weather was pleasant, the dining room was set up on an open air deck with small tables scattered around the floor. They walked into the hum of subdued voices, overlaid by the music from the orchestra. Eddan guided her through the line and then chose a table for two. While they ate, he told her about the history of the castle and temple.

There seemed to be something very familiar about his description of the two places. "Have you been there before?" Naomi asked him.

"No. As I told you, I did considerable research in planning this trip. My wish is for you to enjoy yourself."

Suddenly Naomi yawned. "I'm sorry" she apologized. "All of a sudden I feel sleepy. I don't understand. I slept well last night."

"Don't worry. A nap will be good for you. Tonight there is an after-dinner dance. You will feel fresh and ready to have some fun."

Solicitously, he led Naomi back to her cabin. At one point, she nearly stumbled and stood still, shaking her head. "I don't understand," she mumbled.

He opened the cabin door for her and waited until she came back from the bathroom. The last thing Naomi remembered was Eddan standing beside her bed, pensively frowning down at her.

When she awoke, it was already evening. She felt refreshed. She went to knock on Eddan's door. It opened immediately as though he had been waiting.

"Why didn't you wake me?" Naomi asked. "It's already eight o'clock."

"Oh, we're in no hurry. How do you feel?"

"I feel great. I'll get dressed, then, knock again."

Before she could close the door, he said, "Wear the emerald green gown. It will look great on you."

After closing the door, she paused thinking, that's not what I had in mind. She had planned on wearing another gown. How did he know I have an emerald dress? Aw what he heck. I do look good in emerald green. It sets off my auburn hair.

When they arrived at the main dining room, it was full, couples were already dancing in the next room. When the waiter arrived, Eddan, without asking what she would like to have, ordered their dinner and wine. After the meal, for a while, they watched the people and Eddan commented on some of them. I guess he met them while I was asleep, Naomi thought, almost resentful.

Seeing the frown, Eddan quickly asked, "Would you like to dance?"

Not wanting to appear peevish, Naomi replied, "I thought you would never ask."

He led her onto the floor and expertly guided her into the rhythm of a slow dance. Later they went to the casino. He lost; she won.

* * * *

It was late morning when Naomi finally awakened. When she looked at the clock, it was past eleven. I'm acquiring bad habits she thought and stretched, wondering what Eddan was doing. After she had freshened up and dressed, she decided to knock on his door, but it opened as soon as she stepped toward it. Must have ESP

"You look rested," he said. "How about brunch?"

"Since I missed breakfast, I think that's a good idea."

They spent the afternoon on the sun deck swimming, sunbathing, and reading. After dinner, Eddan suggested they make it an early evening since tomorrow they were going sightseeing.

* * * *

Punctual, at seven, Eddan knocked on her door. "Naomi, it's time to get up. It's going to be hot today, so wear something light with comfortable shoes. Also, a hat if you have one."

Still sleepy, Naomi grumbled, "Worse than a nanny."

His solicitousness was slowly getting on her nerves. He seemed to be making all the decisions before she could voice her own. Within half an hour, she was dressed and having a leisurely breakfast. At nine, all those who wanted to go on the tour began to assemble at the lower deck. Twenty minutes later, everyone was loaded onto buses. Eddan contrived to get a window seat for her and during the trip into the city, pointed at different sights and commented on the conditions of the houses and streets, their style and how old the city was.

"You know, you could have been the tourist-guide," Naomi commented, though, not too graciously. Her head ached slightly and she really wished to be alone. She began to resent the constant drone of his voice, aware of a deep depression weighing her down. Her mouth felt dry and she was constantly licking her lips. Once when she peered sideways at Eddan, she caught his harsh eyes watching and she wondered.

The day's agenda was the Citadel. Looking up at the hill, Naomi remembered she had already seen it. When she and her parents had first come to Sarpedion, naturally, they had gone on sightseeing trips.

The driver parked the bus at the bottom of the hill. There was a loading area already crowded with other buses, empty and waiting for their passengers' return.

After exiting the bus, Naomi stood a little off to the side, waiting. There was a lot of clatter and chatter as the people stepped off the bus and reformed into little groups of acquaintances or families. As

Naomi moved a little further away, she spotted Eddan searching for her.

"I thought I'd lost you," he said, joining her. "We're supposed to divide into two groups . . . I guess by age. The guide said that the older people will make the trip up to the Citadel in two stages."

Naomi recalled the steep climb.

When the guide was sure his flock was complete and gathered around him, he gave the signal to begin their ascent. The road wound upwards, twisting and turning. Trees lined both sides of the road, providing some shade. Halfway up was a cove, and many people, especially those with children, wanted a pause before restarting the climb. After a twenty-five minute rest, they went toward the approach ramp into the Citadel.

The Citadel itself was surrounded by thick walls built of heavy, rough-hewn stone. The massive fortification wall clearly indicated its defensive aspect. Once through the main gate, they entered an inner court surrounded by the remnants of buildings with empty windows staring down at them. Inside one of the ruins was a room with a hearth in the center. It had a round roof, supported by four columns and was still intact. The rooms were stark with unadorned walls. The guide surmised it had once been a hall of state. It probably was lest austere when there were pennants and tapestries on the walls, Naomi thought.

The living areas were more pleasant in contrast to the bare rooms. There were faded frescoes adorning the walls, their hues still discernible, and in niches stood a few well-preserved sculptures. There was also a bathhouse, very much intact. The inner court had contained a fountain. After being shepherded across the courtyard, the group came to what must have been the soldiers' barracks and the stalls where animals had been kept. There was also an armory.

Before viewing the underground store rooms, they were given a short break. Naomi used it to get away from Eddan for a breathing spell. He had been close at her heels all morning long. Even when she struck up a conversation with people walking beside her, he interrupted and diverted her attention to something they were passing on the road.

Finally alone, she walked up to the wall and taking a deep breath, leaned on the parapet to look out over the land. It was beautiful. Mostly deep, richly green farmland laid out in clear discernible tracts.

"Isn't it nice and peaceful here?" Eddan said, coming up beside her.

Naomi, slightly irritated, turned her back to him and looked at the buildings. "Wonder who built this place," she mused more to herself than Eddan. Then taking notice of him and just to be saying something, she asked, "You remember the guide mentioning that the older part of this palace was already ancient and in ruins before this newer addition was built?"

"I bought books about its history. If you're interested, you could read up on it when we are back on the ship."

"Maybe," she said curtly.

"Do you still have your headache?"

"Yes. It hasn't gotten any better, and now I'm thirsty."

Before he could stop her, she strode away and found a stall that sold bottled water. Before she was able to take a drink, Eddan grabbed the bottle and tipped it away from her mouth.

"Naomi, drink slowly. Don't gulp."

He ensured that in the beginning she only sipped the water. After a while, her headache went away.

"Do you know what caused my headache?" she asked him, her tone slightly suspicious.

"You were probably a little dehydrated."

"I hope you're right."

At the end of the tour, they rode the bus to a restaurant that served what the guide assured them was authentic national cuisine.

It was already late when they arrived back at the ship. After a short rest, Naomi went to the women's sauna, a place she knew Eddan couldn't follow her.

She was again rethinking her decision to come on the trip. There was something about Eddan that was bothering her, but she couldn't put a finger to it. She decided that as soon as they came to a city with an airport, she'd fly back by herself.

Chapter Four

The next day, the ship was far out into the bay. Eddan, true to his promise, brought her books about the Castle's past. The stories were interesting. Soon, Naomi, lying in a lounge chair on an upper deck, became caught up in its history and the mythology surrounding it. She had forgotten all about Eddan, so was annoyed when he suddenly loomed in front of her and snatched the book away.

She gazed up to see that he was wearing his bathing trunks. Eddan was slender, but well built. Not bad looking in a swimsuit.

"You have been reading long enough," he said brusquely. When she gave him a questioning look, he mellowed his tone a little and asked, "How about going for a swim?"

"If you say so," she told him.

She headed to her cabin to change and had to step around a young couple coming down the long, narrow corridor. The girl seemed radiantly happy and they were holding hands.

The girl gave Naomi a friendly smile and asked, "Are you enjoying your trip?"

Naomi returned the smile and replied, "The ruins yesterday were interesting, weren't they? I have been reading up on it."

The young man arched an eyebrow. "Reading?" he asked in disbelief. "I'm not much for reading books on a trip. I like to have fun, and there's a lot happening on the ship," he told her.

"We have seen your companion around, but not very much of you," the girl said. "There was a game this afternoon and tonight there's a play. Are you going?"

Naomi looked mildly surprised. "Probably," she said slowly. She hadn't known about any games or the play.

Suddenly Eddan appeared in the corridor. "Naomi! I'm waiting," he said sharply. "Oh, hello," he told the couple when he realized they were talking to Naomi. The two stared at Eddan, and Naomi glanced at the girl and colored slightly at his rudeness.

There was a momentary silence.

"Did you enjoy the game this afternoon?" the man asked Eddan, trying to smooth over the awkward silence.

"Yes, it was interesting," Eddan answered abruptly as a flicker of annoyance crossed his face.

"You went to watch a game?" Naomi asked surprised.

"You were engrossed in your book."

Naomi, vexed at his presumptuous attitude was about to reply when the girl asked, "Will you be at the wedding?"

Before Naomi could ask questions, Eddan quickly said, "Yes, of course, we wouldn't miss it."

When the couple was out of earshot, Naomi asked, "What wedding and why didn't you tell me there was something going on. I would rather have watched that game than read."

"But I thought you were interested in the book. Hurry up. Let's go and change," Eddan urged.

Naomi gave him an exasperated look and went into her cabin.

That evening, after dinner, a theatrical company presented their play and to the guests' delight many of the audience were used as extras.

* * * *

During the night the ship had made the next port.

Soon after breakfast, everyone assembled again on the lower deck to board a bus. This time the objective was the Acropolis. The history of the Acropolis indicated that it had first been inhabited nearly three thousand years ago. In the beginning, it had been a settlement, then a fortress, and eventually a religious center. Later, a temple was added and the city grew around it. The city was still viable, but the temple and its surrounding buildings were in ruins.

The only parts of the temple still standing were the outer columns and remnants of the walls. The structure once contained two rooms. In the inner room, was a dais and on it sat the statue of a god. He must have once been of huge proportion, but, alas, his face and most of his upper torso were gone. On the still standing walls were frescos, depicting people carrying offerings, as well as battle scenes. Naomi didn't have the heart to tell Eddan that she had already seen this, too. Eddan became disgruntled at what he took as her disinterest in his efforts to explain the Acropolis's history. "You don't still have a headache?" he asked her sharply.

"No. I'm feeling better than I have for some time. I don't know what's the matter with me? I never have headaches, and I never have felt so disoriented before. I think when I get back to Vasilika I'm going to see a doctor. Something's not right."

"Yes, it might be a good idea," Eddan agreed.

"What's next on the agenda?"

"We will be shown some old folk dances. I hope you will be more interested in that."

Once their guide was sure everyone was accounted for, he led them to an open plaza. Waiting for them were an orchestra and young people in colorful costumes. After everyone was seated, the music struck up a quick and lively tune and the dancers streamed out onto the tiled courtyard.

Naomi stiffened. She knew this tune and the dance. Years ago, a troupe had performed it on Novalis and taught it to anyone who wanted to learn it. She had danced it many times with the special person who had once been a big part of her life. She sat dry-eyed and tense. More then ever she wished for the cruise to be over. It was late when they arrived back at the ship. Naomi felt so tired and drained the only thing she wanted was to go to bed.

* * * *

When she awoke the next day, it was late afternoon and Naomi felt such a great weariness, and the grief over Caleb's death triggered by the dance yesterday welled up again. It was hard for her to concentrate on anything. She went to the top deck with a book. It lay in her lap; she had no energy to focus on it. Her eyes gazed vacantly out over the sea. For once she was alone. Only once did Eddan check on her and brought her something to drink.

It was just before sunset when Eddan returned, elegantly dressed and escorted her to her cabin.

Spread across her bed was a white dress and veil. Satiny shoes stood beside her bed. She looked at it all with complete detachment. Her mind didn't register the purpose of the layout.

"Naomi, it's time to get dressed," Eddan told her gently as he initiated the undressing. With his help, she dressed and looked at him. He looks nice; must be quite an affair to be clad in such a slick Tuxedo. Before they left her cabin, Eddan handed her a glass of water. "Better drink this now, since you're thirsty," he told her.

I'm thirsty? She didn't think so, but obediently drank the water.

When they arrived at a large ballroom, the Captain was standing on a podium saying something about a pleasant duty to perform and that all the paperwork had been completed before coming on board.

Naomi had no idea what he was talking about, so she just stood next to Eddan at the back of the room. When the Captain finished, he waved for them to step forward, indicating a place in front for them to stand. There were three more couples similarly dressed. Suddenly, the orchestra began to play and several people she hadn't seen before lined themselves up beside the couples.

I didn't know we were going to be in the play. I wish Eddan would tell me about these things. Wonder what kind of play this is where extras have to wear wedding gowns. Not like I'd be getting married. Once there was a time, but . . .

The Captain was asking her something, but since she didn't know the script, she just looked at him.

"Naomi Atossa, do you understand what I'm saying?"

"Yes," Naomi said, and after a pause, "I do . . ."

"I now pronounce you husband and wife."

That was silly. I hope Eddan isn't taking this serious. *S*he almost giggled.

Afterwards, there was a dinner and then a dance. Naomi had no idea how and when she made it back to her cabin.

Next morning, she awoke with a nasty hangover. Swallowing, she shuddered at the foul taste in her mouth. She groaned, then, rolled out of her bed to go to the bathroom. The door to Eddan's room was closed.

Must have been one hell of a party; I don't remember a thing. She stopped and thought for a moment. Weird dream; she had dreamt of having married Eddan. That would be more like a nightmare. First thing in the bathroom she went for the mouthwash, gargling several times, then, took her shower.

While she was toweling herself dry, she noticed a light blue diaphanous nightgown and a lacy peignoir hanging on the door. Where in the world did these come from? There was nothing like that in her wardrobe. Most of her things were sensible and comfortable, although she had several beautiful gowns she once wore to Embassy functions.

Naomi shook her head and immediately wished she hadn't. "I hope Eddan has a bigger hangover than I do, so I won't t have to look at him," she mumbled.

Wrapped in a towel, Naomi went back into her room to dress. She heard voices on the other side of her door. Then there was a sharp rap. Before she could duck back into the bathroom, the door flew opened and Eddan, wrapped in a silk dressing gown, swept in pushing a cart, a steward behind him, reached to close the door.

"Good morning! Today is breakfast in bed, my dear," he announced loudly and cheerfully. When the door clicked closed behind him, he looked at her towel and asked, "Where's the pretty nightgown I bought you?"

"You mean that's mine?" Naomi asked, gesturing at the bathroom door.

"Of course. It's my wedding present to you. I hope you didn't forget. You are now my wife."

"I . . . I'm wha?!"

"You're my wife. We got married last night."

Naomi looked at Eddan and in disbelief shook her head. "I must have been more drunk than I thought," she mumbled to herself. She turned to Eddan, "What do you mean, married? I don't remember getting married. All I know for certain is I have one hell of a hangover, and I can't remember a thing from last night."

"You must have taken your medicine for motion sickness with the alcohol. You know, it's never good to mix medicine with alcohol," Eddan scolded her.

"Medicine? I never took any medicine," Naomi protested.

"Yes, you did. The first couple of days on the ship you were sick. I went to the ship's doctor and got some pills for you."

Naomi stared at him, her dark hazel eyes wide with astonishment, thinking, I have never in all my life been seasick. I wish my memory wasn't so fuzzy. I don't remember half of this trip.

"Let's put the nightgown with the peignoir on and then have breakfast in bed. I rented an opera to watch. Since there is nothing going on today, we can make it a nice lazy day, just the two of us."

When Naomi looked at him distractedly, he shooed her into the bathroom with, "Hurry up before the food gets cold."

A very confused Naomi slowly closed the door behind her. This has to be a nightmare. She was totally disoriented, trying to concentrate on what she remembered. Absentmindedly, she slipped into the nightgown. When she walked back into her room, Naomi stopped for a second, struck by how incongruous it was that Eddan should be sitting in her bed. He had one of the breakfast trays across his knees and the other one was on a cart beside the bed.

"Come, Naomi, let's eat," he coaxed, patting the space beside him.

To reach the place he was patting, she had to go around the bed. While she was making a place to sit, he turned the screen on.

Naomi began watching the opera while she ate. After a few minutes she realized she had already seen this one and didn't like it. The plot was too obscure and mystical for her taste.

Later, when Naomi tried to remove the tray, Eddan said, "I will ring the steward for it," and rang the service bell. When the steward came in, Eddan told him to put the do not disturb sign on the door.

As soon as the steward left, Eddan fluffed her pillows and had her lean back.

As the opera unfolded, Eddan became engrossed in it.

Left undisturbed and lying back on her pillows, Naomi's mind raced. She tried to piece things together. There was something very, very wrong. No time did she remember ever agreeing to marry Eddan. She thought to confront him, but some inner sense warned her that he could be dangerous. He must be deranged, or obsessed, or something. She began to be afraid of him. As soon as possible, she was going to talk to the Captain.

Somewhat calmer from her decision, she fell asleep during the production. When she awakened, the steward was in the room again, and this time laying out dinner for them. Somewhat disconcerted, Naomi thought, it's already evening? Another day has slipped by without my being aware of it.

After they finished eating, Eddan suggested she take a scented bath to make her feel better. "Maybe it will help you relax. It's probably only a tension headache."

Naomi shrugged. They weren't doing anything, so why not she thought and went to run the water. Eddan came in with a small bottle and after unscrewing the lid, let her try its scent. Heavenly, she thought. After Eddan left, she disrobed and allowed her body to sink slowly into the bubbles. Without her hearing him, Eddan had come in; she didn't notice him until he had sat down on the rim of the bathtub. Before she could protest, he began massaging her temples with an aromatic oil and then worked on the back of her neck and shoulders.

"Lean forward and I'll wash your back." She complied, reluctantly and with caution. When he had finished and had left, she noted he had left the door open.

Naomi had just finished drying herself when Eddan appeared again at the door.

"Come, I'll give you a full-body massage."

She looked dubious but he only smiled and went to the bed, pulling the covers back. With her towel draped around her, she went to the bed and gingerly sat on the edge.

"You don't need the towel anymore," he told her. Lifting it up and off, he let it ceremoniously drop to the floor. Silently directing her to lie down on her stomach, he began by massaging her shoulders and back, then slowly moved down to her buttocks, her legs, and to her feet. Then he lay down beside her and pulling her halfway across his body began massaging her breasts, and finally his fingers slowly began to work farther down across her lower abdomen.

Naomi wondered at her lassitude, and was surprised at her body's response. Must be the hot bath, she thought. Nevertheless, she enjoyed his ministrations. When his mouth wandered below her belly, he stopped her protest with his hand on her mouth. Sometime, during the night she was startled out of her sleep. She was lying on her stomach and a weight was holding her down. There was a grunt.

"Eddan!" she called out alarmed.

"It's all right, Naomi. I'll be careful."

Suddenly, a sharp pain made her cry out, and he responded in surprise, "I didn't know you were a virgin."

* * * *

Again, she awoke late. There was the gentle rocking of waves breaking against the ship. We're in port? She was astonished. Last night, they had been in the open sea. I wonder where we are this time. Hopefully there's a city close by, with an airport. Her thoughts reviewed what had happened last night. Her body quivered with delight, but her mind shuddered in dismay. Still, she remembered nothing about the wedding. In her mind she was certain that she had already decided to somehow annul the marriage, but for now, it was consummated. Oh God, this is appalling!

"Are you awake?" Eddan's voice, deceptively mild, called from the door.

When Naomi turned her head, she could see him leaning against the doorpost watching her in a way which always made her feel curiously uncomfortable. Her first reaction was to pull the bed cover up to her neck.

"Where are we?"

"We're on an island called Eubea. The ship will stay here for a few days to refurbish, so we're having a holiday. No sightseeing. Only lying on the beach and soaking up the sun. We also have a hotel room, so you need to pack. We're supposed to be off the ship by noon."

Naomi looked at the clock, shocked to see that it was already eleven. "Why didn't you wake me?" she chided Eddan, throwing the cover back.

"Aw, you were sleeping so beautifully. I hated to disturb you."

Naomi went into the bathroom, and this time she locked the door before taking a shower. Under the water, she gave way to her anger and frustration, and suddenly pummeled the wall. Finally the tears came. She had totally lost control over her life and had no idea how to get it back.

Startled by a loud knock on the door, she shut the water off.

"I'm coming," she called out. When she entered the room her things were packed and her clothes laid out for her. She dressed and staring at his closed door, she hoped he hadn't heard her cry.

There was another knock and the steward's voice reminded her that she had to be off the boat by noon. She opened the door, "I'm ready," she told him and snatching her suitcases, walked out without telling Eddan.

There was a sigh of relief. No Eddan, she thought as she walked down the ramp and boarded the shuttle-bus to be taken to the hotel. At the hotel, her name was called and she almost failed to respond. Naomi el Halugh, she thought, as a wave of despair swept over her.

She acccpted the key that was handed to her. As soon as she arrived at her room, she stepped through her door only to see Eddan standing in the adjoining door. He didn't say a word, only turned and disappeared into his room. He had anticipated her actions and let her know that she hadn't got away with a thing. She found his triumphant look to be insufferable.

Angrily, she slammed her suitcases down on the bed, and taking the key, went down to the lobby and strode out of the hotel. For more than an hour she walked along the beach until she felt calmer.

Realizing she was thirsty, she decided to go up to one of the stands dotting the beach to get something to drink. When she reached into her pockets, she discovered she had no money. Shocked, she stiffened, her whole body turned cold at the sudden realization that without money, she would be helpless.

Naomi raced all the way back to the hotel. Arriving upstairs, she discovered Eddan was gone. He was not in his room, nor anywhere in the hotel. Slowly she walked back to her room, then, methodically went through her luggage and then his. Her checkbook and credit cards were gone. They were not with her things, nor with his.

Naomi sat down on the edge of her bed, her mind too numb to think.

What is happing? Why? Nothing made sense. Every train of thought she managed to grasp, dissolved into chaos. Her chest felt heavy and constricted, and her hands and feet stung like pins and needles.

Time slipped by. When she noted the sun slanting through the window, she wondered how long she had been sitting there. Sighing deeply, she rose from her bed and went to look in the mirror. Her face was ghastly. She looked around the room and suddenly shuddered. She didn't want to stay in it any longer and decided to go downstairs without waiting for Eddan.

There was a small table in the far corner and she walked over to it and sat. When the waiter came, she ordered and absentmindedly began to eat. Her mind was busy again with reviewing the past several days. Lately, she had lost all sense of time. It felt like a month could have gone by. Everything seemed to be eclipsed and fragmented since she had come on this cruise. She realized now, that there had been days of which she had no memories. What has happened to me? What had Eddan done to me? She needed to keep a diary with an entry for every day. She rose and then quickly sat down again. She had no money to buy a diary. Just then she spotted Eddan, seemingly pleased with himself as he sauntered into the dining room, his hands in his pockets. When Naomi looked closer, she noticed he was wearing a new suit.

"Sorry I'm late," he drawled, and pulled out a chair. As he sat down, he continued with a cocky grin, "Guess what? There's a big university on Eubea and I went to check it out."

Naomi knew he was going to launch into a long speech and interrupted him bruskly with, "Eddan, where's my checkbook and my credit cards?"

His voice became a little short when he said, "But dear, with your new status as a married woman, you needed your name changed. Besides, I will give you enough money to buy what you need."

"But what about my account at the bank in Vasilika?"

"I had it transferred to our account after we were married."

"But, it's my money, not yours . . ."

"My dear Naomi," he interrupted stiffly, "It's a joint account. I see no need for you to have a separate checkbook. Like I said, you will have money enough to buy what you need."

"Do you know I didn't have any money to buy myself a drink of water?" She looked at him, her hazel eyes brimming with angry tears.

"If you hadn't run out of the room in such a hurry and reminded me, naturally I would have given you some. Now let's drop this subject. Since you're finished eating, shall we go up to the rooms?"

Eddan rose and walked away, not even waiting for her. When she made it to her room, the door was open, but Eddan was nowhere to be found. He had disappeared without letting her know where he was going and still, she had no money. Her heart sank heavy with despair, a feeling she was becoming more and more familiar with. Before going down for breakfast the next morning, Naomi reminded Eddan that she was broke.

"What would you need money for?" he asked petulantly. "I set up a tab where you can order what you need."

"I would like to buy some personal items, if you don't mind," Naomi said tartly. When she assumed a waiting attitude, he finally went to get his billfold. Under her scrutiny, he counted out a few bills. When she didn't take them, he sighed heavily and added a few more.

Breakfast was a strained affair, eaten in total silence. Once, during the meal, she stole a surreptitious glance and saw guardedness in his eyes and something else. Naomi shivered. Just before he rose, he told her that he was going to be gone all day and for her to have fun.

After he was gone, she sat very still. Her sagging shoulders felt heavy as she pulled them up and sighed. As soon as she was sure he was really gone, she went to the hotel's small curio shop and purchased a map of Eubea. The island was larger than she had thought, and to her dismay, the university she had hoped to get legal advice from was on the other side. Also, after asking the clerk, she found that there was no embassy of any kind there.

Enraged, she let loose some choice words and garnered a few curious looks.

Damn she thought! I'm checkmated every way I turn. She called the Embassy in Vasilika. It was a holiday. It was closed.

Her only hope left now was to talk to the Captain. When she made it to the ship, she was informed by the guard that he had left.

"Left!" Naomi was at the edge of hysteria. "When will he be back?"

"Lady, he is with his wife and kids for a few days off."

"It's urgent, please! I must speak with him."

"He will be back before the ship leaves."

"Leaves to where?"

"Parma. This is the end of this tour."

Her lips trembled and she took a long, deep breath. "Thank you," she managed to say to the guard, and walked away with a cautious sigh of relief.

Thank God. This nightmare may have an end. At least in Vasilika I have friends. Feeling better than she had in a while, she went sightseeing and bought herself the few items she needed, including a diary.

When Eddan didn't come home that day or the next, she wasn't worry. One more day and then I will be going back to Vasilika and don't care what Eddan says or does. I'm going home to Novalis.

Chapter Five

Today was the day to see the Captain. When she awoke, the sun was shining brightly through the window. Startled, she looked at her clock. It was already past noon. The ship! She leaped out of bed. Through the window she could see that the ship had departed. She panicked. Her heart nearly stopped. Thunderstruck, she stood with her hands and forehead pressed against the window pane. What happened? I remember setting the alarm last night.

When she turned back into the room there was Eddan sitting on a stool with a taunting grin on this face. He had been watching her the whole time.

"What's the matter?" he asked her solicitously, his tone mildly deceptive.

Shaking, she groped for the bed and sat down on its edge, a rushing sound in her ears. She looked at him like a pleading child. "Eddan, what's going on? What happened? The ship; it's gone. Weren't we supposed to go back to Parma today?" she asked him tonelessly.

"No, Naomi. We're staying on Eubea. I transferred your records to the university here. In two days, intersession will start. We better hurry and get settled," he said with false cheerfulness.

She gaped at him as though he had suddenly sprouted horns. All the blood drained from her face. She took a shaky breath and asked, "We're not going home?"

"No, Naomi. I have been looking quite some time for a better job and this university has offered me one. I gave this matter a considerable amount of thought and decided it would be stupid to pass it up. You can continue your studies here as well as back there. Now pack. We are being picked up in twenty minutes."

Her mind was racing. What could she do? Something warned her to go along for now.

"But what about our tickets?"

"I cashed them in and rented a house. You will like it. I already bought furniture. It should be delivered this afternoon. So we better get going. Our things from Vasilika will be coming in a couple of days as well. I contacted friends and they are sending it all."

"You have been remarkably busy," she said and turned away from him to hide her tears. Listlessly, she went about packing while her restless mind worked. What can I do to get out of this?

Eddan had gone to settle their bill.

Finished with the packing, she collected her suitcases and rode the elevator down. When the doors opened, Eddan was standing in front, waiting for her. Instead of helping her with the suitcases, he turned and strode briskly to where his luggage was leaning against the checkout desk.

"Do we still have time?" Naomi asked.

"Why?"

"I have to go to the bathroom."

"Why didn't you go upstairs?"

"I didn't want you to have to wait."

He looked at his watch. "All right, five minutes."

She went into the bathroom and heaved a sigh of relief. There was a phone. She called the Dream Boat and asked for the Captain. It's urgent, she told the operator.

"The ship has already left harbor."

"Please, please connect me. I need to talk to him. It's very important."

Her voice must have communicated her desperate situation, as the operator complied.

When the Captain came on the line, she spoke clearly, "Captain Dasha, this is Naomi Atossa. I was on your ship with Eddan el Halugh. Please contact the Embassy of Novalis in Vasilika. The Ambassador knows me personally and is expecting me to return with your ship. Eddan el Halugh has cashed in our tickets, so I'm forced to stay here. I have no means of getting back. I have no money. Tell them what happened and for them to come and find me. Eddan el Halugh is working at the University of Hilo."

"I thought there might be something amiss. I will contact the Ambassador personally."

"Thank you. I have to go before he becomes suspicious. Please, don't forget me. I need your help."

Eddan did look suspicious when she came out of the bathroom.

"I had to stand in line," she fabricated.

When their transportation came, it was a bus. Before boarding it, Eddan came back with two bottles of soda, and handed her the one with the straw.

"I thought you looked thirsty," he said, and took a sip from his. "It's going to be a long day."

The bus ride across Eubea from Styra to Hilo took more than six hours. During most of the ride, Naomi felt drowsy. At Hilo they changed to a grubby looking bus and two hours later arrived at the end of the line. The area looked desolate and definitely rural.

Eddan was busy with the suitcases just before the bus left. Naomi looked apprehensively around and asked, "Where in the world are we?"

"I told you I rented a house. Now pick up your luggage and follow me," he told her sharply.

As they turned off the highway onto a dirt road, Naomi's uneasiness grew as she trudged behind Eddan. Soon they came to a fork in the road and

Eddan took the narrower path. Coming around a bend, Naomi gasped. A dilapidated shack-like house stood mostly hidden in the midst of an overgrown meadow.

The suitcases dropped from Naomi's hands as she gaped. Shocked, she asked, "Is that the house you rented?"

Eddan neither answered, nor stopped, continuing ahead. When she caught up with him, he was already in the house, heading down a narrow hallway.

Naomi dropped her luggage and looked around the room. "At least the inside looks clean. I guess you could call this the living room," she mumbled to herself.

The room was small and dingy, smelling of mildew. The floor was made of roughly hewn wooden planks. There was a couch that sagged in the middle, its fabric faded. One of the two chairs was propped up with a block of wood for a leg. There were shelves; probably book shelves. Peering down the hallway, Naomi could see four doors. Two were on the right, a third to the left, and the last at the end of the hall she surmised to be a closet. She was still surveying the place when Eddan came down the hallway and picked up one of her suitcases. He opened the door to the left and put it inside.

Distrustful, she followed him. The room was small with no windows. It contained one narrow bed, a desk with a chair and a nightstand. There were no sheets on the bed, and the mattress was stained.

"The bathroom is across the hallway. It's connected to my bedroom. You can use it to take a shower or bath. For anything else, you will use the small bathroom behind the kitchen."

He walked out, slamming her door.

Naomi sat down on the bed, too stunned to react. After some time, she pulled herself together. She looked at her suitcases and decided to unpack later. She slowly rose and stepped out into the hallway. The house seemed eerily silent. The other two doors were closed and there was no sound coming from either of them. When she opened the door at the far end, it was a linen closet containing towels, sheets and blankets.

She fixed her bed, putting two sheets between herself and the mattress. Finished, she stepped out into the hallway again and into the bathroom. There was no sound coming from the other room. Cautiously, she opened the door. The room was empty. It had two windows and a large, wide bed covered with a luxurious comforter. The furniture looked new.

Ah, there is the new furniture he was talking about, Naomi thought grimly. She took a deep breath, then, walked through the house in search of Eddan. He was nowhere, so she walked around the outside and still no sign of him.

She reentered the house through the back door into the kitchen, which was quite small, but at least it had a refrigerator. Opening its door, she found that it was running, but empty. Then she opened the cupboards. There were a few dishes and pots and pans, but no sign of food. Off of the kitchen was a utility room with a washer and dryer and an ironing board. The other door was the aforementioned bathroom. It contained a toilette and a sink with a mirror above it.

Naomi returned to the living room. There was still no sign of Eddan. Probably went to get some food, she hoped. She was growing hungry, but decided to take a shower before he came back, so went into his bathroom. She locked the door and then the connecting door. She was about to rinse the shampoo out of her hair when she was suddenly slammed against the wall.

"Thought I was gone, my sweet," he said and laughed. "Bend over and back your ass toward me, you bitch," he hissed at her, grabbing her hips and pulled her against him. Then he raped her.

When he left, Naomi collapsed in the bathtub, the water still running. She was panting hoarsely. She pummeled the bottom of the bathtub with her fists in a mounting rage. Suddenly the water came cold. He had turned off the hot water at the tank.

She rinsed her hair in the cold water, dried herself and then went to her room. Her suitcases were gone and also the clothes she had laid out. Wrapping the towel around herself, she went to the door, but it was locked.

"Eddan!" she yelled, pounding on the door. "Open this door. Let me out."

There was no answer.

She threw herself on the bed and cried at her sheer helplessness. She was far out in the country and nobody would hear if she screamed. During the night she was jolted out of her sleep by Eddan throwing himself on top of her, and this time she did scream. He only laughed and she could smell a faint odor of fish on his breath.

As he lay panting and spent on top of her, she asked, "Eddan, why are you doing this to me?"

"I don't have to explain a damned thing to you, nor answer your damned questions. The only thing you have to do is spread your legs when I tell you." With this he rose, he kneed her bed roughly and left, locking the door behind him.

She awoke the next morning tired and heavy-headed. The door stood open. Wrapping her towel tightly around, she peered cautiously down the hallway and listened. The house was silent, but she had learned to distrust it. Eddan's bedroom door also stood open. When she looked in, the bed was rumpled and empty. Sunshine was streaming through his windows.

She made her way to the kitchen and then to the bathroom assigned to her. Eddan was nowhere to be seen. She went back to the other bathroom to clean up. When she returned to the kitchen, she gave a startled shriek when Eddan snatched the towel off.

He slapped her hard across the face and threw her on top of the table. As he was assaulting her, he began to croon, "Sex in the shower, sex in the bed, sex on top of the table. Next time, maybe I'll stick your head in the toilet. No, I'll wait until I'm ready to drown you. Won't that be novel?"

"Eddan, why are you doing this to me?" Naomi asked.

He slapped her across the mouth. "I told you not to ask questions. I will slap you every time you do. Now fix something to eat."

"Eddan, please, give me my towel back," Naomi pleaded.

"Nope, you're going to run around naked. That's the way I like it."

She avoided looking at him as she walked over to the stove. On the counter were eggs and bread. He had brought coffee and butter.

Naomi fixed breakfast and then felt foolish sitting naked at the table. When she continued to sit, he barked, "Wash the dishes; they don't clean themselves."

She went to the sink and began running the water. When she stooped down to get the soap from under the sink, he said, "Bitch, when you bend down, I want your ass to come up. No need to be lady like."

She was almost finished when he left the kitchen and came back in with a broom and dustpan.

"Now sweep the floor."

She tried to sweep up the dirt behind him, but he turned around and laughed. "No, no, no," he said, shaking his finger at her. As she bent down, he bent over her back and fondled her. When she flinched, he slapped her across the butt, then, ran his tongue up her back.

He left again and this time came back with a mop and a pail. He watched her as she mopped the floors and fixed the beds. When she began cleaning his bathroom, he slammed the lid down on the toilet and threw her on top of it.

"I promise I won't drown you, yet," he assured her, affably. When he was finished, he ordered her to get out.

Naomi went to the bathroom behind the kitchen to clean as much of him from herself. The face looking at her from the mirror was grey. She felt sick. All she wished for at that moment was to throw up. Before she touched the knob, she stood frozen, her senses tuned to any noises in the house. She could hear water running. A little while later, there were footsteps and someone moving down the hall, then, a door slammed. Looking out through the bathroom window, she saw Eddan walking away from the house, well-dressed, heading toward an outbuilding. Soon she heard the sounds of a motor starting and watched as a small red sports car backed out with Eddan behind the wheel. As he drove past the house, he revved the engine.

There was a shiver of rage and bitterness as Naomi crumbled to the floor, her whole body heaving in uncontrolled weeping. She thought she had only closed her eyes for a moment, but when she raised her head, the sun had already set.

Using the toilet seat as support and painfully slow, she pulled herself up. Her head swam; she was dizzy and hurt all over. Looking down at herself, she saw why. No wonder. I'm black and blue all over. She went into the kitchen. Her towel lay on the floor just where he had dropped it. She made her way to the stove and prepared a small meal for herself.

Suddenly she shivered. The house was getting cold. She put the dishes into the sink, then thought better of it and washed them before going to bed.

* * * *

The next morning she lay in bed listening. The house was quiet. She needed to go to the bathroom. Warily, she forced herself to rise. When she came back, her suitcases where standing in the middle of the floor, and her clothes were laid out on her bed. Everything was the way she had left it two days ago.

You're not going to play with my mind again, Naomi promised herself. Suddenly, she realized she smelled food cooking and hurriedly dressed. When she walked into the kitchen, an old woman stood at the stove.

"Good morning, Mrs. Halugh," she said, cheerfully. "I'm to tell you that your husband has hired me to take care of your house. He said that you were going to school at the University and needed all your time and energy to study." Going over to the counter she picked up two booklets. "He also asked me to make sure to give you your bus fare and your meal tickets for this week. And in the living room are your books and your class schedule. He said he would be home later."

Incredulity and confusion twisted Naomi's expression. "Thank you, Mrs . . . ?"

"Reno. He said you weren't feeling too well and for me to tell you that you should rest. He was ever so nice. He must really love you."

"Thank you, Mrs. Reno," Naomi said politely, keeping her voice bland and void of emotion.

After eating Naomi went into the living room and picked up her class schedule first. She was enrolled for intersession, four hours, so four classes. According to this schedule she went to class every day except mid-week. Her earliest class was at ten o'clock.

Suddenly Mrs. Reno stuck her head through the door. "Your husband also said to tell you that to make your first class you will have to leave about eight. It's a two-hour bus ride to the University. So you just leave your breakfast dishes. I'll wash up. And best if you leave me a note about what you want me to do."

"Thank you, Mrs. Reno, I will."

Going over her class schedule, Naomi picked up the appropriate book and began to read. With a start, she realized that she had read two pages and fallen asleep. Putting the book down, she went outside. Curiosity drew her toward the shed. Maybe she could find something she could use. When she stepped through the still-open door, she found the shed totally empty and clean. Someone had removed whatever was in it and raked the floor.

Naomi decided to explore the area, taking the path that led behind the house. It ended at a virtual jungle. The overgrowth between the trees was so thick it was nearly impregnable. Disheartened, she returned to the house. It still smelled like cooking, so she went first to the kitchen.

"I'm fixing your supper," Mrs. Reno told her. "It's just about finished and you should eat while it's still hot. Tomorrow, I will put your supper into the refrigerator and you can eat it when you come home."

"That will be fine. Mrs. Reno. Are there any other houses around here?"

No Mrs. Halugh. Behind your house are the beginnings of the Marshes and I wouldn't go there. Across the main road are the badlands. Only sheepherders go there occasionally. This is a pretty lonely place."

"Who owns this house?"

"It used to belong to an old man who cut and dried peat to sell. It has been standing empty for a long time. I have no idea who owns it now."

"Thank you. I kind of wondered who would live this far out."

Mrs. Reno gave her a curious look, then went to ladle stew into a bowl. She set it in front of Naomi with a slab of bread and a glass of tea.

When Naomi felt Mrs. Reno was safely gone, she dropped her slacks to look at her buttocks and heard a sharp intake of breath.

"Your husband did this?" she asked shocked.

"Yes, Mrs. Reno, but don't say anything," Naomi told her and quickly pulled her pants up. "Another thing I'd like to ask is how you are paid and who paid for the groceries you brought in?"

"I have an account at the supermarket, and he pays me by check."

"So, there's no way I could get my hands on some money?"

"No. I would like to help if I could, but I'm a widow and I need every bit of what I earn."

"It's all right. I will find a way to get out of here."

"Sorry to leave you like this. I have to run or I'll miss the bus."

Mrs. Reno grabbed for her purse and almost ran from the house.

* * * *

Intersession lasted for six weeks and during all that time, Eddan did not once come home. At the end of the six weeks, Naomi went to the advisor's office to inquire about the next semester's requirements and was told that all her courses had been pre-selected for her.

When she looked surprised, the Professor told her that according to the file, her husband had arranged her schedule. "The reason he gave was that you were visiting relatives and had asked that he register you for your classes. You didn't tell him this?" the professor asked.

"No, and I don't have relatives on Sarpedion; I'm from Novalis."

"I thought so. I recognize your accent. Is there anything you want to change?"

"Yes, my name. It's Naomi Atossa, and I am single."

"But it says here that you are married."

"I don't remember getting married," she told him.

"All right, if you say so. What else do you want to change?"

"If possible, some of my courses."

"Let's see." He turned to the computer and ran through her file again.

Naomi pointed to an entry, "I would like to take a course on Sarpedion's divorce laws."

"And drop what?"

"Criminal Justice. I've already had a class in that."

The Professor typed in the changes and sent them to the next department.

"Now, you need to go the registrar and pick up your schedule."

"Would you do me one more favor? Could you tell me how my tuition was paid?"

Once again he returned to the computer and went through her file.

"You have a stipend and after your tuition is paid the remaining money is to be transferred into the checking account of Mister and Mrs. Eddan el Halugh."

"I see," Naomi said.

"Also, something you didn't know?"

"No. Would you make a note that I asked about the allocation of the stipend? My parents had set this up to pay for my tuition and also for living expenses. Have you any advice on what I can do?"

"You have no access to money whatsoever?"

"No. I have a prepaid bus fare and prepaid meal ticket. I live about fifty miles out of town and have no other way to get around. I have a daily cleaning woman who comes in and she has an account at the supermarket."

"Your husband is Madrian?"

"Yes. But he says he's permanently on Sarpedion and has no intention in ever going back to Madras."

"I wouldn't bank on that. I have no liking for Madrian marital laws. All the rights are on the husband's side. My mother had married a man from Madras. As soon as I was old enough and able, I brought my mother and my sister back to Sarpedion. How did you get to Eubea?"

"It was arranged just like my class schedule, without me. Eddan el Halugh and I were traveling on the cruise-ship, Dream Boat. For most of my time on that ship, I am convinced I was drugged. I don't remember getting married. We came to Eubea for a short stop-over. It turned out he had cashed in the tickets and I had no way of getting home. My credit cards and my checkbook disappeared. I am totally without funds. I tried to place a call to the Embassy of Novalis in Vasilika, but it was a holiday and the Embassy was closed. But I did get in contact with the Captain of the Dream Boat and asked him to contact the Embassy of Novalis for me."

The Professor nodded his head. "I see. You've already initiated your rescue. I will help you, but it has to be after registration."

"I understand. Besides, I need to graduate, so I will stay as long as I have to."

"Let's look at your file, again." He scrolled through it and looked at her credits. "With intersession and this upcoming semester, you could graduate. Let me talk to the Dean and I will tell him your story."

"I hate to asked favors. I have no money as you know, but could I make a call to my credit card office. I'd like to report the cards stolen."

The Professor smiled. "Good idea," he told her. "Make the call."

She dialed the mainland office, but when she told them her name, she was immediately put on hold.

"Miss Atossa? I'm the manager of this office and we have been looking for you. Both your credit cards are maxed, and the monthly rate you pay is not enough to cover it."

"Mister Manager, I'm calling to report both my cards stolen . . ."

"That's a likely story . . ."

"Yes, I understand. But I also know the thief. His name is Eddan el Halugh who currently resides in Hilo on Eubea. Check the University for his employment and address."

"Are you sure he is the thief?"

"Yes. He admitted it to me when I confronted him."

"We will take the necessary steps. Where can I reach you?"

Naomi puffed out both cheeks. "I wish it was that simple." She turned to the Professor and asked, "Can I use your office for my mail?"

"Yes, I think that would be safest. Hand me the phone." He gave the manager his name and office address.

As she left her advisor's office, for the first time Naomi felt a twinge of hope. A week before the new semester started, her belongings from Vasilika finally came. As she unpacked her books, she began to leaf through them, checking how much she still remembered. She picked up one of her earliest law books, and as she thumbed through the pages, she found a gold certificate stuck in the crease. She had forgotten all about it. Her father had given it to her on her twenty-fifth birthday in case she was ever in need of money. God, am I ever.

Now she could go back to Novalis. She heard a sudden noise and quickly let the book fall shut on the certificate.

Eddan walked in. "What are you doing?" he asked, casually.

Her whole body reacted with fear and she braced herself and nearly cowered. Eddan noticed it and grinned.

"What are you doing?" he asked, again, with his now familiar, deceptively mild manner.

Naomi breathed in deeply and swallowed the lump in her throat. "Just looking through my old books," she replied and picked up another book.

"Let me see," Eddan demanded.

Naomi handed him the book.

"After you graduate, I will find you a job and maybe let you move into town," he told her graciously.

"That's nice of you," Naomi mumbled. Anger hardened her voice.

"What did you say?"

When she didn't answer, he grabbed her by the hair and slapped her sharply across the face. "My wife is always pleasant and polite. Now, what did you say?"

Naomi altered the tone of her voice and said, "That would be nice."

She began to stack her books into a corner, making sure the one book was out of his sight, when he told her, "Go to your room, get undressed and wait for me."

He was long in coming.

* * * *

Finally, the promised day came for the Dean to give her the oral exam. She had crammed for it all week.

She was grilled for two hours in the morning and one in the afternoon.

When she had finished, she was exhausted, but jubilant. As soon as she had her diploma, she was going to be free of her prison. The dean had advised her to take a room in town. Naomi agreed, but had to go back once more to retrieve her books, or rather the one book. Arriving at the house, she crossed the threshold of the living room and was startled by the presence of two men, seemingly standing guard there. One leaned at the window, and the other moved to push a carton into the middle of the floor.

Naomi froze. Her eyes darted quickly to the corner where she had left her books stacked against the wall. They were gone. Also, her suitcases had been placed in the middle of the room.

Frightened and apprehensive, she asked, "Who are you, and what are you doing here?"

The man leaning against the window replied first, "I am Boufaric, Eddan's brother." Pointing to the other man, "That's his cousin Mustafa. Has he never spoken of me?"

"No. He has never mentioned his family." Pointing to her luggage, "What are doing with my things?"

But it was Mustafa who asked her, "What else do you want to take with you?"

"Take with me? To where?"

"You're going to Madras."

"No, I'm not!" Naomi blurted out.

"Father said to bring Eddan's wife along."

"But I'm not his wife," Naomi stated adamantly.

Boufaric looked at her. "What do you mean?"

"I never agreed to any marriage, and I was drugged at that time."

Boufaric's face changed from incredulity to hilarity, followed abruptly by raucous laughter. He turned to the other man and among one more guffaw, told Mustafa. "Now if that won't amuse Father, I'll eat your socks."

"Please, won't you leave me here? I'm not his wife. I don't love your brother. I want to go home."

Boufaric's face grew contemplative as he scrutinized her. "Naomi, he has registered you as his wife on his papers. Father said to bring you back with him and we cannot disobey."

"Tell him you didn't find me."

"I can't do that, either. It is never wise to lie to him. Something you best remember when you meet him."

Naomi crumbled to the floor and began to cry.

"I'm sorry, Naomi . . ."

"He's coming," Mustafa whispered, as he moved the suitcases and the carton out of sight.

They heard a car drive up and a door slam. Naomi was still sitting in the middle of the floor crying when Eddan strode in. When he saw Naomi on the floor he grabbed her hair and pulled her up. "What's your goddamed emergency that I had to come all the way out here?"

"That's no way to treat your wife," Boufaric tut tutted as he came out from behind the door.

Releasing Naomi's hair, Eddan spun around, turning white. "Wha . . . what . . . what are you doing here?" he stammered.

"Father said it's time for you to come home."

"I'm not . . . I'm not going back to Madras,"

"Oh, yes you are," Boufaric said calmly, nodding his head. "You see, Naomi is already packed."

"Eddan, tell him to leave me here," Naomi pleaded.

Eddan gave her a vicious kick and Boufaric clouted him for it. Naomi looked up at him with a slow growing grin. "I think I'm going to like you," she told him.

"I wouldn't," Boufaric told her coldly. Turning to Eddan, "Get whatever you have to take, so we can get out of here. The police are looking for you."

Eddan looked at his brother and then at Naomi.

"I reported that you stole my credit cards," she told him.

Eddan let loose a string of invectives. "I'm still not going with you, and you can't make me," Eddan retorted, hotly.

"That's what I thought you would say," Boufaric said.

Until then, Eddan had been unaware of Mustafa, who moved quietly behind Eddan and put a cloth to his mouth and nose. There was a short struggle, then, Eddan collapsed to the floor.

"Are you coming or do we have to sedate you too?" Boufaric asked Naomi.

Naomi looked at him and then at the large, muscular Mustafa.

"No," she said, "it would only be wasted energy. But let me write a note to my cleaning woman so she knows I'm not coming back. She can take everything that's left here."

"All right. Do that," Boufaric told her, then followed her into the kitchen.

She wrote to Mrs. Reno that she wouldn't be coming back, that she could have everything left in the house, and to notify the Dean of the Law Department of her departure.

Boufaric read the note. Seeing nothing suspicious in it, he allowed her to put it on the refrigerator door. Back in the living room he pointed to her two suitcases and then picked up the box with her books and papers. Mustafa hoisted the still unconscious Eddan over his shoulder. They exited through the kitchen where a van was parked at the back door. Boufaric first loaded the box and then took the suitcases from Naomi, and Mustafa dropped Eddan onto the floor.

"Get in," Boufaric told Naomi.

Naomi complied with alacrity and was somewhat relieved when Mustafa climbed in behind her. Paradoxically for her, Mustafa was a bulwark against Eddan. She didn't relish being alone with him when he woke up.

They rode for what Naomi judged to be three to four hours. During all this time, no word was uttered between them. When the van stopped, Boufaric opened his door and climbed out and Naomi realized they were at an airport. He helped Naomi out of the van and pointed to a small airplane. Without a word, Naomi went to the plane and climbed up the steps. Suddenly she heard a yelp of pain and looked back. Eddan was stumbling from the van holding his jaw.

I guess Boufaric clouted him again, Naomi thought, feeling great satisfaction.

The plane seated four people plus the pilot and co-pilot. Naomi sat in the window seat behind the pilot. When Eddan came down the aisle and stopped beside her, she turned her whole body away from him.

Mustafa pointed to the seat across the aisle. After Eddan was seated, Mustafa shackled his hands and then his feet to the seat. When Mustafa turned toward her, Naomi quickly held up both hands and said, "No trouble."

"All right," Mustafa said and took the co-pilot's seat.

When Boufaric passed down the aisle, he paused by Eddan and checked his shackles, and then looked at Naomi. "You could play stewardess."

"I don't mind," Naomi told him. "After we're in the air, I'll fix some coffee."

She watched as Boufaric checked off his list and then contacted the tower. The permission for departure was given immediately.

After they were in the air, Naomi went to the niche that held a coffee pot and a microwave. She made coffee for all the men except Eddan, and then one for herself. Seated in the window seat again she looked down at the sea of clouds and the blue sky above, but after a while, she dozed off. She was awakened by Eddan complaining that he had to go to the bathroom.

Mustafa unshackled him so he could walk, then, stood guard at the open door.

"Damit, close the door," Eddan grumbled.

"I don't think you have anything I haven't seen yet," Mustafa baited him.

"Close the door!" Eddan shouted at him.

"Hey, Naomi, come here and see if he's got something we don't know about," Mustafa called out.

Naomi stuck her head over the seat. "I don't think so. Besides what he's got is not worth mentioning," she told him.

Mustafa guffawed.

Naomi was silent during the rest of the flight, watching the three men. Several times she caught the expression of stark hatred in Eddan's eyes as he glared at Boufaric and she thought how these two were so unalike. No one would ever guess that they were brothers. Where Boufaric had assurance and rough manners, Naomi noticed that Eddan was shifty. It's weird that I hadn't noticed it before. I wonder what's with all that viciousness toward him. She shuddered inwardly. What kind of family was she going to be dropped into? She knew never to show fear. She had honed this skill in dealings with Eddan.

* * * *

At the Space Port, Naomi hoped that they would run into a security guard or policeman. She had steeled herself to raise hell if necessary, accusing the men of kidnapping her. But when they entered the terminal, it was nearly empty, probably only used for loading cargo. She saw very few people, and being hemmed in between Boufaric and Mustafa gave her very little leeway to move.

Shortly after arriving, they boarded a shuttle bound for the Space Station orbiting Sarpedion. Coming through a gate, Mustafa flashed a badge. To Naomi's raised eyebrow, Boufaric informed her, "He's an interstellar cop."

"Nice perk, having one of those in the family," Naomi quipped, resigning herself to go along for the time being. She continued to plan ways to escape, but there never seemed to be a safe or clear opportunity.

At the space station, they immediately boarded a cargo ship that also took on passengers. During all this time Eddan had been hand-cuffed to Mustafa.

Onboard, Boufaric showed Naomi to a small cubicle.

She stopped at the door and peered in. There was only one bunk. "Kind of small," she told him worriedly.

"But it's all yours."

When Naomi gave a very audible sigh of relief, Boufaric grinned and told her, "He'll be confined to his cabin, and if he doesn't behave, to the brig."

* * * *

The next morning she had just left her cabin when she was abruptly intercepted by a crewman who politely asked her to return to it immediately. Naomi's instant impression was, I must be a prisoner. Frightened, she complied.

Shortly thereafter, Boufaric came to her cabin.

To her concerned question, "Am I a prisoner?" he chuckled. "No, Naomi, but you're on a Madrian ship. It is not wise for a woman to go unaccompanied and in any state of undress."

Glancing down at her clothes, she asked, "What do you mean by undressed?"

"This ship is Madrian, not Sarpedion. Women are not allowed to show all that skin," he told her, looking at her bare midriff and bare legs.

Helpless, she lifted both shoulders. "But what am I to wear?"

"I'll be back in about twenty minutes to pick you up and will bring you something appropriate." He returned thirty minutes later with a grayish garment draped over his arm.

"What's that?" Naomi asked suspiciously, wrinkling her nose.

Boufaric replied somewhat curtly, "Just put it on."

It was called a qamis, a garment that covered her from neck to toe in cloth and long sleeves. He also handed her a scarf to cover her head. "Now you look civilized and can come with me to eat breakfast," he commented, dryly.

Not in the least appeased, Naomi heaved a heavy sigh as she meekly followed Boufaric to the mess hall.

Before he deposited her back at her cabin later, she asked him if she could have her books back, and if there were any language tapes in Madrian, thinking, I am going to learn this language before we land on Madras. He brought them to her without a fuss.

Chapter Six

The trip lasted seven long weeks with nowhere to go and nothing to do. She was told to stay in her cabin. The only person she saw during all this time was Boufaric who only came to take her to the mess to eat. During the long days and hours, she studied the language tapes and reread her law books. She also began to exercise in her cabin.

Never once did she catch sight of Eddan.

After the ship docked at the Madrian Space Station, Naomi was instructed to stay in her cabin until sent for. It was an hour later when Boufaric came to pick her up. They exited the ship and walked down a narrow corridor similar to the one on an airplane. At its end stretched a reception area and the gate to the shuttle. Naomi had hoped there would be some formalities to go through and thought, maybe someone I could alert to my plight. But they merely walked through the gate.

I guess it was all taken care of before Boufaric came to get me, Naomi thought bitterly, as she boarded the shuttle. There had been no chance to flag anyone for help. Tired and feeling hopeless, she boarded the crowded shuttle, noting she was the only woman on board.

She looked for Eddan and spotted him sitting beside Mustafa. This time, he was unshackled. She met his hostile stare with a feeling of dread thinking what's going to happen to me? What kind of family is this? The treatment meted out to Eddan left her very apprehensive.

Naomi turned toward the window and watched as the shuttle was unfasten from its moorings. She experienced what seemed to be a short free-fall and then they swerved away from the Station. Suddenly, a huge planet loomed up at port-side where Naomi sat. Within forty minutes, the shuttle landed. Naomi was told to remain in her seat while the aisle cleared. A short time later, a woman came down the empty walkway. She seemed to be in her early thirties, and though covered by her qamis, she appeared slender. Her features were regular, her eyes dark. She wore her hair in two long, dark-brown braids. Without uttering a word, she motioned for Naomi to follow. When Naomi stepped through the hatch, she was met by a cool, brisk wind and took her first deep breath of the fresh air. She saw that all the other passengers had left. At the bottom of the step, another van waited. A slight nudge on her shoulder meant to move on.

In frustration, Naomi's fingers tightened into a fist. There was no escape.

A few steps down and she was in the van, being motioned to go to the very back. The woman indicated for her to take the window seat and then sat down beside her. The only other passenger in the van was Eddan. When he looked back, Naomi noticed he had a black eye. She quickly ducked her head to hide the contempt she felt for him. Boufaric and Mustafa were accompanied by an older man. There was very little conversation between the four males, only what seemed necessary. The woman beside Naomi was silent throughout the journey. After leaving the Space Port, the van entered a busy four-lane highway. Naomi, engulfed in her misery, was barely aware of their turns or stops. For most of the trip, she kept her back to the other woman.

They only stopped a few times to go the restroom and once to eat. The men drove all that day and through the night, at intervals switching drivers. At all times, one of the men sat next to Eddan. It was mid-morning when they left the highway and entered a two-lane road. They turned onto another road, then after a mile or so, entered another road leading to a heavy, metal gate between stone pillars.

Boufaric turned in his seat and pointed to the entrance. "Naomi, this is Oran, This is our home."

After a twenty minute drive, they reached a sprawling compound surrounded by a stone wall. They drove through a vaulted entrance and stopped in a cobbled courtyard. The woman motioned for Naomi to follow. When Naomi exited the van and stood to look around, the woman quickly pulled her scarf up to cover her head.

At Naomi's look of surprise she advised her, "You're a woman and you must go covered at all times when you are in a public place."

"You can talk after all," Naomi said, giving her a slightly crooked smile.

The woman only looked at her. "Now, we must go to the women's part of the house. Please follow me."

They crossed the courtyard and entered through a massive door into a foyer with a tiled floor. Naomi had barely time to glance around, though she noticed that it was Spartan, but spacious. She was led two floors up and at the end of the hallway, the woman opened a door and indicated for her to enter first.

"This is a guest room. It is for you to live in until the Master decides. My name is Mari and I'm bid to take care of you."

"Thank you, Mari. Are you allowed to talk to me?"

She turned to Naomi with a scrutinizing look. "It is not wise to be flippant in this place," Mari warned her.

"It was not asked lightly. I was referring to information. I don't want you to get into trouble."

"Your name is . . ."

"Naomi." She was going to add Atossa, but held her tongue.

"Here, it is always good to be sensible and do as you are told," Mari said sternly.

"Thank you, Mari," Naomi said meekly. "Is there anywhere I could wash my clothes?" She had been living out of her suitcases and had hand-washed what she could while on the spaceship.

Mari gave Naomi's attire a critical look and suggested, "Take a shower if you like. I will bring something for you to wear. On Madras, women go covered." Naomi was wearing a short skirt and a short-sleeved blouse. Mari, on the other hand, had on loose trousers and a long overdress. Naomi simply looked at Mari, then, went into the bathroom. When she came out, fresh clothing was laid out on the quilt, and her two suitcases and the box with her books were standing near the foot of the bed.

A short while later Mari returned and showed her the laundry room. Naomi was repacking her clothes, since she wouldn't be allowed to wear them, when a gong suddenly echoed through the house. She opened the door to peer out and saw a young girl waving for her to follow.

On the ground floor were a kitchen and dining room, and also a large community room, most likely for gatherings. The girl led Naomi to the dining room. Women, four of them, were already assembled around the table for the evening meal. At the head of the table sat a large, heavyset woman, her face bland and impassive, her hair was a mass of light brown curls. Her brown eyes were intelligent as she studied Naomi with unabashed scrutiny.

Good Heavens, the presiding matriarch, Naomi thought irreverently. She stopped at the end of the table and bowed. Slowly raising one finger, the woman pointed to the chair where Naomi was to sit. Once seated in her designated place, the clatter of dishes started and the food was passed from the head of the table to the end, and Naomi was seated at the end. When the food finally came down to her, she took what little was left.

After dinner, everyone rose. Now what? Naomi thought.

Mari touched Naomi's arm, and beckoned her to follow. "The mistress said that you might be tired and want stay in your room to rest. I will come tomorrow morning and show you what you need to do."

Standing inside her door, Naomi thanked Mari and watched her walk away. There must be a way to talk to her. There were so many unanswered questions and the uncertainty and silence everyone maintained had given her an ominous feeling.

Her room contained a poster bed, a nightstand, and a large wardrobe. Next to a window stood an easy-chair and a small table. There were two plain throw rugs, one in front of her bed, and the other in the middle of the floor. With no pictures on the walls, the room seemed impersonal, telling her nothing of its inhabitant's likes or interests. She looked out of the window, and just below was a vegetable garden. No flowers.

Naomi shuddered. Will this nightmare never end? The heavyset woman had made her especially uneasy. She had ruled from her chair with languid and watching eyes the entire time. I wonder what goes on behind that deadpan face?

Naomi sat in her chair, leaning back to think over the past month and a half. On the spaceship, she had seen nothing of Eddan and was glad of it. Boufaric had kept his distance and Mustafa had been taciturn and silent as usual. In the beginning, she had tried to elicit information from Boufaric, but his only comment had been you'll find out soon enough. I hope Mrs. Reno went to the Dean with my note. At least it would alert the Embassy that I've been moved again.

At the end of her musing, she decided that if asked questions, she would supply the least possible details about herself, especially any mention of her notifying the Embassy of Novalis. In the back of her mind she kept a glimmer of hope. At least I still have the gold certificate. Someday, somehow, I will get away from here.

When no one came, she prepared for bed. During the night she dreamt about Eddan and then with a sudden jolt sat up. Now she knew what had been bothering her about him from the very beginning. All the time she's known him he seemed so unreal, because he's been acting, playing some sort of role.

Taken aback she laid down and let her mind play back to the time when she had first met him. He had been the considerate and helpful friend, interested in all she was doing. But now she realized that he had never really been concerned for her. During the first days of their marriage, he had projected the caring husband . . . yes, until I was isolated and helpless. But still, what reason did he have to pick on me for his purpose, whatever that was?

* * * *

This was her first day at Oran. Sitting up in bed with her arms wrapped around her knees, Naomi let her eyes move across the room to the window. It was still dusky, but outside the new day was dawning and it was overcast. It is as dreary as I'm feeling. She tried to keep the dismal thoughts at bay, but was overwhelmed with the anger and fear at her circumstance and her sheer helplessness. With a shaking hand, she pushed back her auburn hair, dreading another day and what it might bring.

A knock on the door startled Naomi and she froze. Relief flooded her face when Mari walked into her room and turned the light on. Naomi saw that she carried a garment draped over her arm.

"I think this will fit you," she said, as she hung it over the footboard of the bed.

Naomi eyed them. "Thank you, Mari. But I have clothes of my own."

There was a quirk of a smile. "The way you dress would cause a riot."

"Why?" she asked, slightly irritated and frowned.

A tiny smile touched the corner of Mari's mouth. "You show too much skin. This will do much better."

Naomi picked up the baggy slacks in one hand and the long overdress in the other, sighing in resignation. "I guess on Madras you conduct yourself as a Madrian," she accepted and put on the garments.

Mari watched her dress and thought, Poor child; you're nothing but skin and bones. Mari felt genuine concern for her, for what little she knew of Eddan, whom she had met for the first time when he returned from Sarpedion, had not been very comforting.

Just then, the familiar gong sounded.

"Time for breakfast," Mari informed her.

Again, the Matriarch presided at the head of the table and what food made its way down to Naomi grew scant. After breakfast, everyone remained seated. After a while the Matriarch shifted and began calling out names, assigning various duties to the women. When she came to Mari, she said, "Have . . ."

"Naomi," Mari supplied.

". . . make herself useful." She rose ponderously and left, followed quietly by the other women.

"The Master doesn't like lazy women. Everyone has to be busy. So, clear the table and help in the kitchen," Mari explained.

Obediently, Naomi cleared the table and then helped wash the many dishes. She noticed a broom standing in the corner, so she swept the floor. Later, she went into the common room and helped a young girl vacuum, then tidy up the rest of the room.

She didn't mind the work, it helped pass time and kept her from worrying too much. But her mind went over her impressions of Boufaric. She wondered at his refusal to deviate from his father's orders. Then, there was Mari telling her not to be glib . . . always do as you're told. She was about to ask what else she could do, when Mari walked in with a qamis over her arm and a scarf in her hand.

"The Master wants to see you now," she told Naomi. "His name is Hadjar, and he is addressed as My Lord. Do not forget that."

Naomi felt a sudden dread and went cold all over. She had already gathered from the whispers and demeanor of the women that the Master was not taken lightly.

The room into which Naomi stepped occupied the whole of the floor space at the east side of the house. It had floor-length windows around most of the room and a huge, free-standing fireplace. The ceiling was cathedral style and the room was sparsely furnished. Only one huge divan was pushed against the only wall that was windowless. On it sat Hadjar and next to him the fat Matriarch, watching placidly as Naomi crossed the floor. As she neared the divan, she observed Hadjar from under her lashes, trying to read his face.

Hadjar el Halugh was well built, but slender, with a hawk nose. His black eyes were fierce and malicious. His hair was grizzled but the brows were still jet black and thick. He had an arrogant, intemperate mouth.

No, not an easy person to please, Naomi thought as she stopped in front of the divan and dangerous too. She made a short bow, first to him and then to his wife, then waited to be spoken to.

While his eyes appraised her, Naomi's heart began to thump against her ribs. To show fear, she knew, was to be lost. Just then, she became aware of Eddan standing to one side of the divan with Boufaric.

Eddan looked very pale.

When Hadjar saw that she had noticed Eddan, he turned to him. There was a gleam to Hadjar's eyes and a growing curl to his lips when he said. "Why don't you do the introduction?"

Eddan responded quickly. "Naomi, this is my father, the Lord Hadjar el Halugh and his wife, the Lady Saada. Father this is my . . .'

Before Eddan could finish, Naomi quickly interrupted, "My lord, if you will grant me my say this once, I will never mention it again."

"What is it you want to say?"

"My lord," she began making her voice as firm as she could, "My name is Naomi Atossa. Eddan is not my husband."

"But on his papers you are mentioned as his wife," he argued, never even glancing at his son.

"My lord, paper is not discriminating."

"That is a worthy point," he exclaimed. "So tell me how all this came about? How did you two meet?"

Naomi thought for a moment, organizing how to relay the facts to the father of Eddan and Boufaric. She spoke clearly, "It began in a crowded cafeteria. He asked if he could share my table, which was not my table; it was the cafeteria's. After that day, he began popping up everywhere I went. We talked some and he invited me to a concert. Eventually, he began coming to my dorm and helping me with my studies by listening to me explain what I had learned that day. It helped a lot. At the end of the semester, he offered to share two cruise tickets. He said he had gotten them at a good price and invited me go with him. I declined at first, wanting to go home to Novalis. My mother is ill and I wondered why I hadn't heard from her. But he told me the cruise would be only for one week, and it would be a shame to waste the tickets. I finally agreed . . . partly to stop his badgering me. Coming back I would still have had twelve days left before going to Novalis. So I agreed to go on the cruise with him.

I was hustled onto a train, then, hustled onto the boat. Everything seemed to have been minutely timed. This was something I realized only in hindsight. Also, for most of the trip I feel certain I had been drugged, because there were days I have no memory of. Things seemed inaccurate and fuzzy.

Before we stopped at an Island called Eubea, there was some sort of a ceremony and at the time, I thought it was a play. I met a couple who told me about it, so when Eddan brought me a white dress with a small veil, I thought nothing about it, other than it must be a costume of sorts. Somehow I wasn't able to concentrate and work out my confusions. I was so worried I would have to say lines in the play that the Captain's words didn't register. He asked me if I understood. I said yes, and after a pause, I actually uttered the words I do. The Captain's pronouncement of husband and wife did not register until much later. At the time, I was trying not to giggle, thinking something ridiculous about Eddan getting any funny ideas.

When the ship docked at Eubea to be refurbished, we were furnished with a hotel room. Later I found out that he had transferred my records from the University in Vasilika to Hilo on Eubea. My checkbook disappeared and so did my credit cards. I had no access to money. Then he rented a house way out in the country. The groceries were charged to an account he had set up for a woman who came in daily to clean the house and cook for me. I had a pre-paid bus ticket and a pre-paid meal ticket."

When she finished, Hadjar el Halugh rubbed his chin with his left hand while contemplating her.

"You had no intention of marrying my son."

"No my Lord."

"I see." Hadjar el Halugh turned with undisguised contempt to his son, "Now tell her your story."

"I saw Naomi and fell in love with . . ."

Hadjar el Halugh's fist came down on the armrest of the divan. "The real story this time, boy." He looked at Naomi, and said, "Did you know that he stalked you to find out what you were doing and where you lived?"

"No my Lord. I had been very ill and it took all my effort and energy to focus on my studies, and then I was worried about my mother and wondered why I hadn't heard."

"Tell her why she hasn't heard from her parents," Hadjar ordered Eddan.

"I broke into her dorm and took the letters."

Naomi blanched as she gasped for breath. The so-long, held-back rage boiled to the surface and she walked over to Eddan and swinging with both fists, hit him across the face.

She was beyond words as she collapsed onto a cushion before the divan. She buried her head in her hands and rubbed her temples for several seconds, then looked up. Spreading her hands in a helpless gesture, she stared at Eddan.

"Tell her how many letters there were."

"Two."

"And the last one?"

"About her mother's death."

Naomi groaned and crumbled. She forced herself to look at Eddan and then up at Hadjar, and asked, "Why?"

"Tell her what attracted you to Naomi?"

"She seemed so quiet and so docile."

"And so very easy to control," his father derisively finished for him.

Eddan could feel the color of his face fluctuate, and he made a desperate effort to control himself. He hated to be spoken to in this manner.

"Did you know Eddan had studied to be a pharmacist?"

Naomi raised her head and stared at Hadjar. She opened her mouth to say something, then, closed it again. Much was becoming clear.

"Do you wonder why I know all this?"

Naomi only stared back at him.

"I had him watched . . . all the time. His mother was a lily-livered, sniveling bitch. I never liked her. She had no spirit. She connived behind my back to get her weakling of a son away from me. She had highfalutin ideas about him. Naturally, I knew all along what she had planned. So, before she could get him away, I had Eddan mix a potion for me. He never asked for whom." Turning to his son, "It was for your mother. She died the night you thought to have escaped me. She bought your freedom with her life. Get it? She never knew how much you hated her or why."

Eddan stood bloodless and pale; there was no sound. He only gaped at his father.

"You see, Naomi, this fool hates women." Hadjar leaned back on the divan. "He only wants to dominate and degrade them. This fool and his mother thought to trick me," he said. "A fine sport they provided for me all that time. Naturally, I kept tabs on him on Sarpedion. Did you know that while you lived out at that god-forsaken place, he was being kept by an older woman? Like a gigolo. He didn't have a job at the University. But then, he was always lazy. He planned for you to keep him in the style he has grown accustomed to, once you were a lawyer."

During his long speech, Hadjar studied Naomi. But she only sat at the base of the divan, too overwhelmed to react.

"Lord Hadjar, I only want to go . . ."

"I know, Naomi, I know, you want to go home. But you see, as far as I am concerned, you're his wife and I want a grandson."

There was a moment of stunned silence as the color drained from her face. Naomi stared at his eyes, which were now less contemplating and more wicked and resolute. She turned away with a contempt aimed at Eddan. Her eyes spoke for her like you cannot be serious!

Hadjar understood her look and gave a sardonic chuckle as he looked from Eddan to Naomi. "You will move in with Eddan. Mari will help you move your things up to his place." Hadjar leaned toward his wife and patted her on the hand. "And you will inform Mari." Turning to Eddan, "Now go and show your wife where she is to live."

Naomi balled her fists in helpless rage. Mutely, she glared at Hadjar. When she looked at Eddan, her eyes glinted and she shuddered. Her movements were awkward as she rose. Without waiting on Eddan, she walked out of the room. Once outside, she refused to look at him. Silently, she followed him to the west wing and up to the second floor.

Eddan's apartment consisted of a living room, bedroom and bath.

Naomi stared at the overly furnished room which seemed to close in on her. Still standing at the door, she looked at Eddan and shuddered. He was extremely pale as Naomi regarded him stonily. With a derisive glance, Naomi walked past him and into the bedroom. It contained one large bed. She gaped at it. Oh no, not again.

On one side of the room, the wall was taken up by a huge wardrobe and on the other side stood a chest of drawers. She opened the doors of the wardrobe first, finding it full of Eddan's things. With rising wrath, she jerked his clothes off the hangers, then went to the dresser and emptied out all the drawers. Rolling everything into a bundle, she heaved it into the living room and threw it on the floor. Without acknowledging Eddan, she went back to the bedroom and slammed the door behind her.

She sat on the bed shaking.

Soon, Mari came in with two male servants carrying Naomi's suitcases and the box with her books. Mari stared in surprise at the heap on the floor and then at Eddan. The men barely suppressed their grin when he pointed mutely to the bedroom.

When Mari walked in without knocking, Naomi jumped off the bed, assuming it to be Eddan. Her pinched face relaxed as she told the men to put the luggage and the box in the bottom of the wardrobe. When Mari moved to unpack, Naomi told her, "Just leave it."

Once they were gone, Naomi began to pace. She was so infuriated by the total disregard shown her. Suddenly everything welled up and she couldn't bear staying in the room. She walked heavily out of the apartment and out of the house. She took a path along the fields that led toward a small hill. When she arrived at its crest, she found a bench, where to her surprise, Saada was sitting. Saada's hands were folded over the top of a walking stick as she gazed out over the surrounding valley. She took no notice of Naomi when she sat down beside her.

After a short time, Naomi said, "It's beautiful here," but Saada only grunted.

They sat long in silence.

"Tell me your story, Naomi," Saada finally asked.

Naomi regarded her, then, took a deep breath. "Between us?"

"Only between us."

"I grew up with a friend. We were always together. People called us the inseparables. Together, we began to study law. We were going be partners and open a law firm. That we would marry was taken for granted. Then he was killed in a traffic accident. I went into shock. I was ill for a long time. Then my father was transferred to our embassy on Sarpedion. So we moved there. I was urged to resume my studies. In the beginning, I didn't care to study law again, but I couldn't get interested in anything else. Eventually I entered the law school on Sarpedion. When I was at the University of Vasilika, I immersed myself in my books and tried to take every day as it came. I took very little notice of anything else. Then my Mother became ill. There was no cure and she wanted to go back home, so my parents left. And then there was Eddan. I couldn't get rid of him. He was always showing up, without invitation. Soon it was easier to accept him, than fight his constant attention."

Saada grunted. She began pointing out places down below, the large area of groves and paths and meadows. "See the narrow track going over that hill? On the other side is my parents' estate."

"You mean you grew up around here."

"Yes."

"Then you knew Hadjar before you married him?"

"My father knew him. Hadjar wanted me as his third wife. When my father refused, he threatened to implicate him in a crime. In order not to have his name and family ruined, my father complied. I was sixteen, then. Before I left my parents' house, my grandmother told me never give your heart, never show fear or any emotion, no anger, no hatred. Be obedient. Do as he says, no matter what. Her final advise was to make myself indispensable. I have obeyed her injunctions ever since, and I am still alive."

"What happened to his first wife?"

"She bore him a daughter and on his father's orders, he killed the baby in her presence. Hadjar's father had wanted a grandson. She picked up the dead child and came up here and threw herself down these cliffs. Since then, Hadjar never comes up here. Eddan's mother was his second wife and Mari is his fourth. Mari also made herself indispensable; she is his housekeeper. She has never borne him a child. I keep the estate books."

The women sat in silence for a long time. When Naomi rose, Saada said, "This conversation never happened, but if you're confronted about it, we spoke of the valley and I told you where I used to live. I will tell them that you are not very talkative."

Without a glance at Saada, Naomi returned to the house.

Saada sat contemplating, knowing she was putting herself in danger. However, another male heir did not fit into her plan. When she chose Mari for Hadjar's wife, she and Mari agreed that there would be no children. Boufaric would be the sole heir and he was soon coming of age. Saada was suddenly roused out of her reverie as Boufaric emerged from behind her.

"Help me up," she demanded, in her surprise, her voice sounded curt.

"Did you have a good conversation?" he asked, scanning her face. But as always, it was unreadable. Long ago, he had learned to read her cues. She wanted no questions asked, but he needed some indications should Hadjar query him.

She scrutinized him, not knowing how long he had been standing behind them. "Somewhat. I told her where I used to live. We talked about the valley."

"Did she tell you about herself?"

"No. She seems very closed mouthed." Thumbing her stick on the ground, she requested, "Now, help me get home." Boufaric took her arm. He knew her portly appearance was no hindrance and wondered at her sudden need for assistance.

Instead of going to her office when she arrived home, Saada went to her room and took to her bed.

Chapter Seven

On her way back to the house, Naomi pondered what Saada had said. She was just crossing the inner courtyard when Hadjar suddenly loomed up in front of her.

"Did you have a good conversation with Saada?"

As Naomi looked up at him she tried to make her face as expressionless as possible. "Not really." And after a slight pause. "Women can sit together without discussions or arguments. It was peaceful up there and I was tired. But Saada did mention that she grew up across the ridge."

A tiny smile curled his mouth. "So you did talk."

"A few words were exchanged, but mostly, we enjoyed the peaceful view and fresh cool air."

"Humph," he said, and abruptly walked away.

No one paid her much attention when Naomi entered the women's common room and sat by one of the windows. Mari, sewing in one corner of the room, acknowledged Naomi with a nod.

Later, Boufaric entered. "Did my mother complain that she wasn't feeling well?" he asked Naomi.

"No, she said nothing to me about it."

"Why do you ask?" Mari wanted to know.

"When she came home, she went straight to bed."

"She did what!" Mari exclaimed. "She has never done that before. I'll check if there is something she needs." Mari put down the sewing and hurried off. She needed to know what was going on.

Boufaric sat close where he could observe Naomi, but she ignored him and kept her attention focused outside the window.

Saada was absent at the evening meal.

After dinner, Naomi helped Mari clean up and since she was not invited to stay, she went up to the apartment. Thank god it's empty. Eddan's clothes had been picked up, and when she checked inside the wardrobe, it only contained her things. She shut the bedroom door, jamming a chair against it. She had no intention of sleeping with Eddan. Before she drifted off to sleep, she thought she heard him pull and twist the knob.

* * * *

Upon returning to the house, Saada did what she knew others would very likely notice, but she needed a space of time with no interruption, so she could think and plan. When Hadjar had told her he was calling Eddan home, she was suspicious, because she knew he had no liking for this son. As far as Hadjar was concerned, Eddan was a spineless waste. When she saw Naomi, yes, that made sense. Naomi was intelligent and probably a fighter. So different from what she imagined Eddan's wife would be. Saada had decided early on that she was going to help Naomi get away from Eddan, but for a reason of her own.

Saada's smile was mirthless. Naomi presented a threat to her plans. She had raised Boufaric to be cautious, but not afraid of his father. She had educated him. Boufaric would soon turn twenty-five, of legal age to inherit, and none of Hadjar's brothers could claim the estate. It was time for Boufaric to take over Oran. She had only three months to plan it all. As far as she was concerned, Hadjar's days were numbered. Naomi, if she managed to get away, might be just the catalyst to trigger Hadjar's possessiveness which would work in Saada's favor. There were still many unknowns, but Naomi could be worked in, if handled correctly.

Suddenly there was a knock on her door. Saada cringed. She had asked to remain undisturbed.

"Saada?" Mari asked, coming into the handsomely furnished bedroom.

"Is something wrong?" Saada asked, raising her head off the pillow.

"No. You're not ill?" Mari asked, worried. Saada was her hope to freedom. It had never been voiced, but the implications that it would be so, were there. When she first came to Oran, she had been very apprehensive. Watching Saada, she soon deduced that she cared nothing for Hadjar. Mari also had recognized a design behind everything Saada did.

Saada had trained her to take care of the household and the task of taking care of Hadjar had also fallen to her. Saada only took care of the books. Since they worked in different spheres, there were only the necessary contacts between them.

"I just overexerted myself," Saada told her.

Mari looked at her. Saada never exerted herself. So that was not it.

"Mari, get acquainted with the housekeeper from the Embassy of Novalis."

"Naomi?"

"Yes."

There were steps in the hallway. The door flew open and Hadjar strode in. "What is it I hear about you being in bed?" Hadjar bellowed.

"Hadjar, dear, I pulled a muscle in my back."

"If you would lose some weight, you wouldn't have that problem. Just look at skinny Mari who never has any trouble, except not being able to give me a son."

"Sorry, Hadjar," Mari said meekly, thinking, I'm afraid to think what you would do if you knew. When Saada had obtained her as Hadjar's fourth wife, she had been frightened, knowing his appalling reputation. Saada's brother was a doctor, and they both had gone to him. He had performed a partial hysterectomy, agreeing that Oran was not a good place to raise a child. He knew about Hadjar's first wife and there were suspicions about the death of his second wife.

Mari turned to Saada, "I'll bring a hot water bottle. So you just stay put," she murmured and quickly left the room.

"You will instill in Naomi how important it is to bear a son, and soon."

"Yes, Hadjar, it would be nice to have grandchildren," she agreed with him, speaking evenly.

"Humph," he grunted and suspiciously eyed her unruffled mien. I wish I knew what went on behind that moon face. If she was not so good at keeping the books . . . I don't know what I ever saw in her and her fat rump, he thought in disgust, and without another word left the room.

When the door slammed, Saada bit her lip. He didn't like fat woman. After Boufaric was born, she had purposely kept the weight she had gained. She also had had her tubes tied without his knowledge. As far as he was concerned, she was getting too old for his taste, anyway. Right now, he was amusing himself with a fourteen-year-old, temporary consort.

"I heard the door slam," Mari said as she came back into the room. "You still want this water bottle?"

"Might as well."

"You will stay in bed?"

"For a while."

"I'll bring your dinner."

Saada watched as Mari left the room. There was never any animosity between them, and often without expectations, they covered for each other. They managed an unspoken alliance.

* * * *

The next morning, Saada was still keeping to her room. After breakfast, Naomi rose and began helping Mari clean the table. When Hadjar came in, he told her, "Today you will help Moshja clean out the stables."

Naomi looked at Moshja. He was small and wiry, with the same dark eyes and beaked nose as Hadjar, and she later learned that he was one of Hadjar's son's by a consort.

Naomi motioned for Moshja to lead the way. Before she left the dining room, she had to pass by

Eddan who had a smirk on his face. Naomi shrugged. She had mucked out stables before.

Later, Boufaric came to check. "Well, well," he said, "looks good. At least you know how to work. Now, you can help Moshja clean the saddles and harnesses."

About noon, Mari brought them something to eat. It was late afternoon before they finished. Naomi went upstairs to wash off the horsey smell and changed clothes. As she was coming out of the bedroom, she was not quick enough when she caught the movement. Eddan grabbed her by the hair and hit her across the face, then slammed her against the wall.

"You bitch. You think you can play me up. You'll soon learn that nobody here will help you. All you have is me. And you better be nice." He was panting and his eyes were dilated. When her clothes wouldn't come off quick enough, he ripped them off. Then he threw her on the floor and himself on top.

When he finally left, she was still on the floor shaking and aching all over. She carefully rose and went into the bathroom and then stayed in her bedroom for the rest of the day.

* * * *

When Naomi appeared at breakfast the next morning her hair was severely pulled off her face so everybody could see her black eye. The women only glanced once, then, continued setting the table. A moment later Mari came in with a young girl Naomi hadn't seen yet. She looked to be about fourteen, very pretty, but skinny with dark hair and brown eyes. When she saw Saada wasn't present, she threw herself into a chair, expecting to be served.

Everyone ignored her.

When Boufaric came in, he stopped and curtly motioned for her to vacate the spot. As he sat down, his eyes fell on Naomi. "What door did you run into?" he asked.

"A five-fingered one," she told him.

Boufaric harrumphed, while his eyes glanced over the food sitting out on the sideboard. "Lessa, get my food," he ordered gruffly.

There was a spark of anger in her dark eyes and she was slow to comply.

Everyone watching considered her a silly girl who gave herself airs because she was Hadjar's youngest consort, and so his favorite for the time being.

No one had yet bothered to enlighten her about Hadjar's true nature.

The next family member to come in was Eddan. He too was ignored. Since no one took any notice of him, he walked around the table and stood next to Naomi. They were all waiting for Hadjar, who was last to appear. When he entered the dining room, everyone switched their attention to him. Boufaric rose from his chair.

Eddan reached for Naomi, trying to pull her behind him. In so doing, he gained Hadjar's attention. He stepped up to Naomi and crowded Eddan out of the way. He took her chin into his hand with a grip that was firm but not harsh, then he turned her face into the light. Hadjar's face darkened as he gave Eddan a caustic glare. Without a word, he went to the head of the table and sat down. Mari immediately began serving him breakfast. Throughout the meal, the atmosphere around the breakfast table failed to grow even partially pleasant. After everyone finished eating, Naomi rose to follow Moshja, but Hadjar said, "Not today. Come with me."

The encounter with Eddan had put Hadjar into a perverse mood. He was irritable and critical of everything he noticed on their way to the stables. Boufaric walked stoically beside him, answering his questions as even tempered as possible.

In the stable yard, Moshja was already waiting for them, holding the reins of three saddled horses.

"This one, mount it," Hadjar ordered, as he pointed to a young stallion. "If you can break him, you can have him," he told her.

Naomi only looked at him. She was not dressed for riding. As she stepped up to the horse, he snorted and became agitated, backing away. He was frightened and obviously uneasy about the weight of the saddle. She held her hand out and let him smell it, then patted his neck. Before mounting, she checked the saddle. Hadjar might not be above a loose cinch, but the saddle was tight, so she took the reins from Moshja. Holding them loosely in her hands, she began talking to the young stallion in a soft voice, stroking the side of his head.

"Mount him," Hadjar barked impatiently.

Remaining calm, Naomi stepped up to his side, and not meeting his frightened eyes, she pushed down on the pommel. When her weight pulled on the saddle, he side stepped.

"Is he broke to a rider yet?" she asked Hadjar.

"No, only to the saddle," Boufaric answered.

She gave Hadjar a scathing look and carefully mounted the horse. He immediately reared and tried to break away. "Easy boy, easy," Naomi crooned as she pulled his head in toward his shoulder. As Hadjar and Boufaric rode off, he began to follow the other horses without Naomi having to prompt him. After leaving the stable yard, they made their way up a rough track to the stud-farm. There were several young foals Hadjar wanted to inspect. One of them caught his attention.

"What do you say to this one?" he asked Naomi.

"He looks promising, long legs and seems to like to run."

Next, Hadjar went to examine two brood mares about to foal. The inspection came off to his satisfaction and his mood lightened. When he spoke to Boufaric, his voice was less strident. After having seen to the horses, they rode out to a pasture with a quick moving stream to check on a herd of cows.

Naomi smiled as she looked out over the grass. There were numerous little bumps dotting the field. Most of the cows had calved, and Naomi made several knowledgeable comments, having spent her summers at the Nunnery's farm.

It was late afternoon when they returned to the house. Naomi was sore, not just from riding, but also from Eddan's assault the day before. When Boufaric made a derisive remark, Naomi returned a poisonous glare.

Stiff, she climbed the two floors up to the apartment. But before she laid down this time she didn't forget to jam the chair under the doorknob.

When she awoke near evening, she was tired and heavy-headed. The room was stifling hot. She went to the window and opened it, hoping for a reprieve from fresher air. When she looked down, she saw Saada in the vegetable garden.

Naomi hurriedly dressed.

"Saada, are you all right?" she asked, as she walked up.

Instead of an answer, Saada said, "Mari tells me your clothes were torn."

"Someone needs to tell Eddan that clothes don't grow on trees."

"At the Embassy of Novalis, would they know your name?"

Naomi looked startled. "Yes."

"Have a very short note ready by tomorrow." Saada inspected the peas in her hand, then, put them in her mouth. Without saying another word, she walked away.

To cover her astonishment, Naomi bent down and tied a loose vine back up.

She stayed in the garden until the gong sounded.

Hadjar was watching as she came in. "Have you seen Saada?"

"Yes, in the garden."

"What did she say?"

"That Mari told her about my torn clothes. I told Saada to tell Eddan that clothes don't grow on trees."

Hadjar's mouth twitched and he gave an angry snort when Eddan came through the door. "How long have you two been married?" he asked him irascibly.

Taken off guard, Eddan stammered, "One . . . one and a half years."

"Why aren't there any children? By the end of this year, Naomi better be pregnant." Hadjar went to the head of the table, and glared at everyone individually, he enjoyed their guarded glances. Only after he sat down, were they allowed to take their seats.

"Saada, you better have a talk with Naomi," he ordered.

"Yes, Hadjar, of course," she said placidly.

The whole evening meal was consumed in uncomfortable silence.

After helping Mari clean up and do the dishes, Naomi went outside to sit in the garden. The heat of the day had dissipated and the air had become mild. Leaning back in a garden chair, she mulled over Saada's strange comment when Eddan suddenly walked up.

"I do not appreciate being embarrassed by you," he hissed.

"Eddan, I don't need to do anything to embarrass you."

"Naomi . . ."

"Eddan, go away. I'm tired and I'm sitting here to rest."

"I'm going to be gone for a few days," he told her.

"Good." was Naomi's curt reply and she closed her eyes.

Eddan hesitated for a moment, then turned and walked away.

Chapter Eight

At breakfast next morning, both Hadjar and Eddan were absent. After clearing the table and washing the dishes, Mari suggested, "If you want, you could come into town with me. I need to do some shopping."

"Do you think I could get some new clothes? All I have is this qamis and one change."

"Yes, that's why Saada suggested you come with me."

Naomi was surprised when Mari climbed into a truck instead of the car. "We need to pick up farm supplies and then groceries," Mari explained.

"Oh, I see," was Naomi's crisp reply, wondering if this had anything to do Saada asking about writing this note.

Town turned out to be Sikar, the capitol of Madras, and situated on a peninsula jutting out into the sea was the spaceport of Madras. As Naomi exited the truck, a space shuttle took off and she stopped to watch it with an aching heart and sighed, if I could only go home, she thought.

At the feed store, Mari left their order.

"While our supplies are being gathered and loaded, we could see about getting you some new attire."

"You know Mari, I haven't had anything new since I ma . . . was kidnapped by Eddan."

"We all know he only cares about himself."

"Where did he go?"

"Eddan, you mean? He went with Hadjar. They will be gone for the day."

Ah, Naomi thought, just for this day. He intends to catch me off guard.

In the dress shop, Naomi selected four outfits, and to her amusement, Mari charged the bill to Eddan's account.

The last stop, before picking up the truck, was a large supermarket. Apparently, Mari was well-known there. The manager personally came to greet her. She gave him a list of the staples to be loaded when she returned with the truck. Next, she went down various aisles to find special items ordered by Saada.

At the spice aisle, Naomi took a small jar from Mari's hand. "We have this on Novalis," she told her, after reading the label.

"This is from Novalis. Saada once had eaten some jellied fish at a friend's house and had really liked them. So every once in a while she asks for it to be prepared."

A lady, also there selecting spices, stopped to talk to Mari like they were old friends. Shock raced through Naomi when the woman was introduced to her as the housekeeper to the Embassy of Novalis.

The note! Naomi thought. She reached into her qamis and palmed it. Searching the shelves she picked up a jar of fruit. With the note concealed under the jar's bottom, she handed it to the housekeeper. "Excuse me, but could you tell me if this might also be the same as on Novalis?" Naomi asked.

"Yes, it is exactly the same," the housekeeper replied.

Several minutes later, Mari said her goodbye and Naomi assured her of how pleasant it was to have met her and to give her regards to the Ambassador.

All the way back to the truck, Naomi hoped it had not been a ruse. From her short time observing Eddan's family, she had gathered that Hadjar was both tyrannical and scheming. One of his greatest delights was playing dirty tricks on everyone. This could be just the sort of trick he would play on her. But somehow, she trusted Saada. Not that Saada cared about her, but her suspicion was, that by helping her, Saada might be following a purpose of her own.

When Naomi arrived back at Oran, she was greeted by Eddan. She felt sure that he had been waiting for her. He was coming through the door of the main house just as she and Mari drove up.

Pointing to Eddan, Mari said, "Naomi, I'll see to the unloading,"

Naomi would rather have stayed to help her than meet with Eddan. But thanks to Mari, she had been warned. Grabbing her packages, she slid off the seat and slammed the truck's door.

Walking up to Eddan, "Didn't you tell me you were going to be gone for a few days," she needled him, while keeping her face as expressionless as possible.

She could see his disappointment at not having gotten a rise out of her.

Trying to appear nonchalant, he shrugged his shoulder. "Oh, no," he told her evenly, "Father only wanted to look at a filly he is considering buying."

Earlier that morning, before Hadjar and Boufaric left for Sikar, Naomi had overheard them laughing. Hadjar had only taken Eddan along to irk him.

"And he took you along for advice?" She allowed a distinct touch of contempt in her voice.

Eddan's face flushed a deep red as he stalked off. He was still angry at having wasted a whole morning listening to Hadjar talk about horses.

* * * *

Several days later, Saada asked Naomi to drive her into Sikar. Every other month, if possible, Saada went to visit her sister for a few days. Naomi surmised it was to get away from Oran. I wonder what her sister will be like, Naomi thought. When they entered the house, the entrance hall proved more spacious than the one at Oran and it had a vaulted ceiling. There was also a skylight and a large potted plant standing beneath. When she heard laughter, Naomi stopped in mid-step.

Azena, Saada's sister, came rushing from the back of the house, still wiping tears of laughter from her eyes. Grasping her sister's arm, she cried, "Saada, I'm so glad you could come. Pia is getting impossible. She complains she is bored stiff since her best friend has married." Azena stopped abruptly when her eyes fell on Naomi.

"Azena, this is Naomi, Eddan's wife," Saada introduced her.

Azena was taken aback. Naomi was not at all what she had imagined Eddan's wife would look like. She had expected someone more simpering and nondescript.

Naomi was also surprised as she looked at Azena's slender figure and benign face and wondered at the dissimilarity between the sisters. Azena's face was open and friendly, whereas Saada's was closed and unreadable. Azena appeared to be in her early forties, with dark brown eyes and strong features that were more handsome than pretty.

"Welcome to my home, Naomi," Azena said, graciously. Then turning toward the back of the house, she called, "Pia, come here. We have a guest."

The minute Naomi laid eyes on Pia, she took an instant liking to her. Pia appeared to be in her early twenties. She was slender like her mother, only a bit taller, with the same dark brown eyes.

Pia grinned when she saw Naomi. "Aunt Saada said she would bring someone my age along, and I'm glad she did. I'm bored to death with absolutely no fun around here," she complained.

"Pia, why don't you take Naomi upstairs? She can have the room next to yours."

"Thanks, Mom. That will be great. We can visit with each other and talk as long as we want to."

Naomi reached to pick up her luggage. "Don't worry about that," Pia told her. "Nash will bring it up." She held her hand out to Naomi, and hand in hand both ran up the stairs.

The first thing Naomi noticed as she stepped into the room was the great big brass bed covered with a flowery bedspread and matching shams. There were several plants in the room and pastel paintings on the walls.

Naomi went up to a landscape, studying it. Since there was no name on it, she asked, "Who painted this?"

"My mother. She's quite an artist."

"I like it. It's good. I have always liked landscapes."

"Well, when you see the rest of the house, there are many more of her paintings on our walls."

Naomi soon discovered that Azena, using her artistic talent, had decorated the house to give it an impression of airiness. The furniture was not as heavy as that at the el Halugh house.

"You like your room?" Pia asked.

Naomi nodded and smiled. "Oh yes, I love it, this looks like a happy room full of sunshine. I will be glad to stay here for as long as I can."

Pia took Naomi by the hand. "And through here is my room," she told Naomi, leading her though the other door.

Naomi stepped over the threshold and stopped. She had never seen anything like it in all her life. The room was a disaster. Pia laughed at Naomi's shocked face and said, "Oh, it gets cleaned up every once in while. Now, let's see what we can do to have some fun," and hopped on the bed.

* * * *

For once, the strain of living with Eddan and his family was at abeyance, if not absent from her mind. Naomi enjoyed her stay at the el Asad household. Only once did she meet Amir el Asad, Pia's father. He reminded her of one of her uncles at the Nunnery, portly and very satisfied with life.

During her stay, Pia took Naomi to several of the boutiques she frequented and introduced her to many of her friends. The boutiques were not only places for women to shop, but in all of them was a corner set aside where pastries and coffee was sold. It was the place to gather and gossip. Pia also took Naomi to a few art galleries and historical sites. Saada's advice was, just charge everything to Eddan's account.

But her reprieve from Eddan only lasted two weeks. One afternoon as Naomi sat on the windowsill playing with a kitten while Pia gave a narrative of their day's exploits. Eddan and Boufaric were shown into the living room.

To Saada's questioning look, Eddan said, "Father has asked that Naomi and I open the winter residence and for Boufaric to drive you back home."

Saada looked at her son and then at Eddan. "It's somewhat early in the season to open the house," she commented.

"Yes, I know. But father wants Naomi and me to spend more time together."

Naomi paled and looked at Saada, who only shrugged. "I guess we need to pack your things and mine," Saada said unperturbed.

During the spring, summer and fall months the Hadjar el Halugh family resided at Oran, but in winter, when work slowed down on the estate, they moved into their townhouse in Sikar. It was a three-storied building on a quiet, tree-lined street. There were two wrought iron gates and beyond them a paved walkway with a half dozen grey stone steps leading up to the house.

When Naomi and Eddan arrived, it was Mari who opened the door.

"Hello, Naomi, come on in. The house is still a mess."

Naomi noted she had greeted her, but not Eddan. "Are you by yourself?"

"Oh no, I have several helpers with me."

"Show me where I can put my luggage and I'll change clothes and help."

Mari led the way through a rather gloomy hall and up the stairs. To the right of the stairs, she opened a door and let Naomi enter first. The room was large, and it appeared to have been used as a bedroom-cum-living-room. Dust sheets still covered the furniture.

"I'll fix up this room and then find you," Naomi told her.

When the door closed behind Mari, Naomi sank to the floor between her suitcases and began rubbing her temples with the palms of her hands. Again, she had been out-maneuvered. She had a horrid closing in feeling like I'll never be able to get away.

When she looked up, she saw there was a floor length mirror on the wall across the room. She didn't like what it reflected: her sitting between her suitcases, with haunted eyes in a sallow face. She sat for a long time. When she finally rose, she mechanically pulled the dustsheets off the furniture and began unpacking her suitcases. Finished, she went downstairs where she found Mari, but no Eddan.

* * * *

It took a week for the servants to clean the house while she and Mari restocked it with groceries and the necessary items a family needed. Eddan was mostly absent. Like Hadjar had said, he was lazy. Then Mari left for Oran. Naomi was by herself, for several days.

Late one evening and still thinking she was alone in the house, Naomi went down to the kitchen to get something to eat. To her surprise, she heard voices coming from the formal living room. They were loud and boisterous. At times, there was raucous laughter, and some of the voices belonged to women.

Curious, she stopped to listen and was startled into an exclamation of alarm by a man walking up behind her. Like Eddan, he was slender with a dark complexion, dark hair and dark eyes.

"Good evening, Naomi," he said in an easy-going manner, and smiled down at her. Wearily she stared up at him.

"Let me introduce myself. I'm Sidi el Asnam, a friend of Eddan. My father's estate abuts Hadjar's. Would you like to join our party?"

"No, thank you. I was just going to the kitchen to get a bite to eat."

He followed her into the kitchen. To her surprise, there was quite a lot of food set out buffet style. Naomi took a plate and selected some of the tidbits and from a half-full pitcher standing on the sideboard, she poured herself a glass of tea. When she came to the oysters, she wrinkled her nose. She had never liked the slimy, fishy-smelling things.

Sidi el Asnam also saw the oysters and bellowed, "Eddan, you idiot. Why in the devil's name do you insist on eating these things?"

Naomi gave Sidi a speculative look, then, quickly moved out of the kitchen as Eddan came in through the other door.

"Sidi lay off. You know they up my potency . . ."

"And make you as mean as hell. You know you're allergic to them."

As Naomi listened, something dawned. Whenever Eddan had raped her, he also . . . and suddenly the penny dropped. He always stank after . . . oysters.

Once she was back upstairs, she locked her door and jammed a chair under the handle before she sat down and took up her book while she picked at her food. She had found a book on Madras history and customs in the el Halugh library. It discussed how women's rights had eroded only within this one century. The restrictions put on them were all in the name of religion. The further she read, the more incensed she became. What a bunch of nonsense. The women went guilelessly along, believing what was preached from the pulpit.

Suddenly, Naomi slumped from the chair. Her last clear thought was, I have been drugged again,

Eddan came in through a secret door and seeing Naomi slumped to the floor, lifted her and laid her on the bed to undress. Then he rolled her on her stomach on top of a pillow with her face turned to the wall. Even drugged, Naomi cringed, expecting his usual onslaught. But it never came. Someone was having intercourse with her, but without the usual battering.

Next morning Naomi woke up with the most agonizing headache she could remember. No, come to think of it, I have had them before. She felt groggy and ill-tempered. After she showered, she went in search of Eddan. She didn't know what she was going to do, maybe threaten him with speaking to Hadjar. She was not going to be drugged again.

But Eddan was nowhere to be found.

* * * *

"Pia, I just want to go to the library. I don't see why you must escort me every time I decide to go somewhere," Naomi complained. "I don't feel comfortable while someone has to wait around for me. Could I just browse and spend some time there? I just need to get out of this house." Whenever she tried to leave the townhouse, Pia or a servant accompanied her.

"But Naomi," Pia placated, "you don't understand; it's not proper for a lady of your status to go downtown by herself."

"But you do it all the time," Naomi parried.

Pia blushed and Naomi understood that this was not it. There were other reasons why I can't go unaccompanied, she thought. "All right, let's go to the mall, then," Naomi temporized.

Since living in Sikar, Naomi's hope was to seek asylum at the Embassy. Now was a good time since Eddan was away. She had thought to sneak out, but it would arouse suspicion, something she didn't want, fearing there would be further restrictions put on her.

One day Eddan was back again. Several times late at night, she heard the door to his room open and close and then his moving around, but he never attempted to come into her room, and by morning he was gone again.

Then late one afternoon he returned, she quickly ran up to her room and locked the door. She had no desire to see him. There were quick footsteps outside the hallway and then she saw the door handle turn.

"Naomi, for god's sake open the door!" he bellowed after a sharp rap.

"What do you want?"

"I need to talk to you."

When she finally allowed him to enter, he tried to take her hands, but she pushed him away. "Cut that out," she told him and slapped at his hand. After putting both hands behind her back, she ungraciously asked, "Now, what do you want?"

"I have made an appointment for you to see a physician.

"What for?" she asked him, suspiciously.

"To see if you're pregnant."

She turned around, staring up at him, growing suddenly irritated. "You must be nuts!"

"Be ready tomorrow morning," he told her.

Next morning, he was at the breakfast table for the first time this month. Naomi was neither thrilled with having to share breakfast, nor with going to the clinic with him. At least at the clinic he would have to cool his heels in the waiting room.

After the examination, while she dressed, Eddan was told that she was definitely pregnant. When the doctor told Naomi, she looked at him, askance. Stunned and fumbling, she groped for a chair. After almost two years of marriage she had thought it was she who couldn't have children. And now this! She was devastated. She didn't want to have Eddan's child. She hated him.

Suddenly, Eddan was the solicitous husband again. She already knew it was a role he was playing that meant nothing. To get away from all the tender loving care, she called Hadjar and asked him if she could come back to Oran, telling him that she would probably feel better in the fresh, country air. Since she was pregnant, Hadjar didn't care if she was with Eddan or not, so he gave permission.

"Tell Pia to drive you home. She can stay at Oran with Saada for a while," Hadjar told her.

Naomi made the call and Pia assured her she didn't mind time away from Sikar and would be happy to drive her to Oran.

Now that she was pregnant, she was released from all duties. Hadjar didn't want her to risk the pregnancy. To fill this unaccustomed leisure time, Naomi took to walking. When Hadjar wasn't around, she rode the young stallion he had given her. Also, after reading the book on Madrian customs and history, she began to rummage through the library Hadjar had on Oran. She found several books on Madrian laws and began to study them.

Chapter Nine

As soon as Hadjar left that morning, Naomi
saddled her horse and rode out of the courtyard. The
hazy and clammy morning was already hot. She could
see the type of clouds forming that meant rain. Naomi
stopped the horse for a moment, trying to decide
whether to continue her ride, and decided to at least
for a short one. For some time, she followed a path
westward that led to a brook. She rode alongside until
it made a sharp bend around a rocky hill, while the
path wandered toward the north.

Naomi reined her horse, undecided whether
to follow the stream or the path. She was gazing
absentmindedly at the grayish water, busily sorting
through troubling thoughts. As far as she was
concerned, nothing had come of the meeting with
the housekeeper from the Embassy. What could
Saada's interest be after all? Of course it had to be
Boufaric . . . His future was her future. Then, this
pregnancy! Naomi shuddered. Mostly imperceptible,
but still, Saada's attitude toward her had changed. If
I could only talk to her, but all Saada's plans seemed

to be indirect and covertly orchestrated. There were undercurrents Naomi didn't understand.

After reading the law books, she now knew that the laws provided no recourse. On Madras, women had no rights. In the beginning, they belonged to their fathers and then to their husbands. It was called protection, cloaked in a lot of euphemism. Yeah, sure, Naomi thought derisively, like my situation. There must be a way out. After a moment, she became resolved. There's got to be a way, and I'll find it. Next time I'm in Sikar. With this small hope, she urged her horse to walk again and was startled by a flash of lightning, immediately followed by giant, heavy plops of rain. She had lost track of the overcast sky.

Naomi spurred the horse to a trot and headed toward the hill, hoping to find an overhang. As she came around the west side, she could see a segment of rock jutting out. Suddenly another horse snorted. With feelings of misgiving, she eased her mount closer. Someone else had had the same idea, and judging from the attire, it was a man. Like she, he was on a horse.

She started to turn around when he called, "Naomi?" When she made no move toward the shelter, he added, "I think there's enough room for both of us." She eased her horse under the overhang and next to him. There was very little light as she peered at him.

"Do you remember me?"

"I don't . . . know," Naomi said slowly, finding the voice familiar. Then it came to her. Back at the house in Sikar. "You're Sidi el Asnam."

Before he could answer, there was a loud thunderclap as the rain came in sheets.

"Yes."

Since the land and hill was part of Oran, she wondered what he could be doing here. She eased her horse a little forward to see his face. "Aren't you far from home?"

"No not really. My father's estate is just across from here. That brook is the boundary."

"Are you on your way to see Hadjar?" she asked, busy with calming her horse each time it spooked after a thunder.

"No. I have been following you."

Taken aback, she asked, "Why would you do a thing like that?"

"To have a talk with you."

Her face tightened. Apprehensively, she asked. "What is it you want?"

"How much do you remember about the evening you met me in Sikar?"

Naomi tried to sit upright and at the same time keep the horse still. "Not much; I was drugged," she said icily.

"I know."

Naomi intuitively sensed that this moment would be a fateful one. Something in Sidi el Asnam's bearing or voice cautioned her.

"Are you pregnant?" he asked bluntly.

Naomi stared back at him. He was watching her and she sensed concern in his voice? She saw no reason not to answer his question. "Yes," she told him.

"Do you know Eddan is sterile?"

She took a sharp intake of breath. "Why are you telling me this?"

"I thought you needed to know."

"No, I didn't know. I thought it was me who couldn't have children."

Then an ugly, monstrous thought entered her mind. I have been used once again. Her memory of that night . . . despite being drugged . . . she had noticed a difference. "It . . . it was you. It wasn't Eddan . . . It was you . . . you had intercourse with me that night."

"Yes, Naomi, I did," he replied, somewhat apologetically.

Shaken, Naomi asked, "Why?"

There was a moment of silence. To Naomi, it seemed an eternity.

"Eddan begged me to get you pregnant, because Hadjar was pressing him to produce a grandson. He was near panic by the time he asked me to help him. He believes that if Hadjar ever found out that he cannot father a child, he would kill him, and I concur. Hadjar's pride would not abide the truth that he produced a son who could not propagate. Since that day, I have been thinking. I have two children of my own, and I love them very much. I don't want any child I fathered grow up in Hadjar's household."

She looked at him. There was hope in her eyes. For a moment, the prison doors were opening, and for that moment, hope seemed possible. "Please would you help me? I need to get away from here. I'm from Novalis and I have been trying to get back home."

"What can I do?"

"Contact the Embassy of Novalis in Sikar and tell the Ambassador about my situation here. And by the way, my name is Atossa. Naomi Atossa. I'm not Eddan's wife and Hadjar knows it. He won't let me go."

Sidi nodded and said, "Hadjar never gives up anything he considers to belong to him. Go home and I will see what I can do."

"I can pay for my trip back home," Naomi interjected quickly before she turned her horse. She rode away through the rain, retracing the path back north toward the house.

She still had her gold certificate, which was now sewn between the lining of her handbag. One afternoon when she knew Eddan to be gone, she had decided to take it out of the book. It was too chancy to leave it there. Someone, out of curiosity, only needed to pick the book up.

* * * *

When Hadjar was finally seriously considering buying the filly, he sent Boufaric to the Asnam estate to look her over. Sidi and Boufaric were sitting under a tree, watching the playful filly, when Sidi suddenly said, "My father has commented several times on why Hadjar called Eddan back, since all here know he openly dislikes him."

"I don't know; maybe just to aggravate Saada," Boufaric said, offhandedly.

"What do you think of Naomi?"

Boufaric was taken aback by the unexpected question and turned to look at Sidi. "Why do you ask?"

"I have met her, in Sikar."

"She has no feelings for Eddan and wants to go back to Novalis." With growing suspicion, he asked, "What are you getting at? Do you care for her?"

"Not in that way," he told Boufaric. "Have you ever wondered why Eddan has never produced a child until now?"

A wild series of thoughts clashed in Boufaric's mind. What was Sidi getting at?

"Boufaric, Eddan is sterile, Naomi is carrying my child."

Boufaric sat motionless, a sickening knot clenching his stomach, waiting for Sidi to continue.

"Eddan is convinced if Hadjar discovered this truth, he'd kill him. Naomi was drugged."

Boufaric's throat was tightening. He stared in disbelief at Sidi. "Why are you telling me this?"

"I want Naomi to get away from here."

"But . . . how?"

"She asked me to approach the Embassy of Novalis, which I did. They told me that her father is on his way here. Naomi has already been in contact with the Embassy."

Boufaric was stunned. He was silent for a long time, mulling over the revelations. Of a sudden he felt cold. Hadjar! He knew how ruthless his father was and so did Sidi el Asnam.

"When will her father be here?"

"In about three weeks."

"That doesn't leave us much time."

When Boufaric arrived back at Oran, he was tired. It had been a long and harrowing day filled with unwanted revelations.

* * * *

Boufaric was on his way to the dining room when he heard a tremendous crash, followed by a loud bellow. Hadjar was on a rampage Boufaric realized, and retreated to the kitchen.

Mari was leaning against a counter, her face ashen.

"What's going on?"

"Oh, Boufaric, Hadjar found out that Eddan rented an apartment down town."

"Where is my mother?"

"Before I could warn her, she went into the dining room."

"You stay in here," Boufaric told her.

When he went through the door, his first sight was Eddan bleeding from his head and face, and his clothes were wet. Hadjar had thrown the coffee service at him. Eddan was dripping hot coffee. Naomi stood in the corner of the room, petrified. The fierceness of Hadjar's anger shook her. For the first time, ever, she looked at Eddan with pity.

Boufaric finally caught sight of his mother. She was leaning silently against the sideboard with her head bowed forward. She had survived many such explosions before and endured them stoically.

Eddan was trembling so violently, he was swaying on his feet. "Father, I was going to tell you," he was saying repeatedly.

"No, you weren't!" Hadjar bellowed. "Like always, you sneak around, you sniveling, misbegotten fool."

When Hadjar paused for breath, Boufaric interjected, "Father, please. Let's go to the kitchen. Mari can fix your breakfast."

Hadjar blinked at Boufaric, his eyes dark and furious. His face was suffused with rage. "Must I now eat my breakfast in the kitchen?"

"Yes, Father, please. Mari will fix you something."

After more cajoling, Hadjar finally agreed.

It was a very odious morning. Hadjar's ill humor descended on anyone who had the misfortune to cross his path.

It was late afternoon before Boufaric found his mother again. She was at the hill, sitting on her bench. When he saw that she was just staring across the valley, Boufaric wondered how often she regretted ever having to leave her ancestral home. Boufaric grunted as he sat down. For a while they sat in silence.

"When are the taxes due?" he asked.

"Not until the end of next month."

"Hadjar will be gone for a while. Why don't you visit your sister?"

"She is going to have guests. Her in-laws are coming."

"That will give you a good excuse to stay for a while longer, helping her."

Saada studied his face, then, nodded. "If you say so. I could also make an appointment to see the doctor about my back."

Chapter Ten

For Lia, the trip home was an endless journey. Although traveling between planets had become easier and the passenger ships more luxurious, there was still the element of time.

In the beginning, Lia participated in the games and entertainment. But during the last stage of the journey, she began to tire more easily. It became harder to maintain interest, even in the activities she enjoyed. She began to stay more and more in the cabin, and Jarrod, to make the time pass, began reading to her.

Finally, the ship docked at the Space Station above Novalis. Since there was no way of knowing the time of landing or how long it would take to go through customs, Lia called her mother to say they would hire a car once the got through the Port of Entry. It was already mid-afternoon the next day when she and Jarrod made it to the Nunnery's driveway which made a wide sweep and Lia watched as the house slowly came into her view. It had stood there almost a thousand years, staid and solid as a bulwark. As they neared the front walk, Lia could see her mother and sister waiting for them on the steps. She easily discerned her mother by the white hair and Mariam's which was more red than auburn. And like most of the Atossa women, both were petite and slender. When the car stopped, Lia's sigh was long as she looked up at the house. She was doing what she had sworn she would never do . . . return to the Nunnery.

Hearing the deep sigh, "Lia" Jarrod chided her as he handed her out of the car. "It's going to be all right," he assured her, his lips gently brushing her cheek. The last time Jarrod had been to this house, he had asked for Lia's hand and been refused. He had only recently become a lawyer; he was young and fresh out of college with few prospects. Lia's mother had entertained other ideas for her daughter.

The Nunnery was the ancestral home of the Atossa. It had become a refuge for widows and tired old men at their journeys' end. But it had also been a safe haven for the young people to grow up among aunts and uncles, siblings and cousins. And some, like Lia's mother, had stayed, married, and raised their families at the Nunnery. On Sarpedion, Lia had been diagnosed with an incurable blood disorder. With care, she could prolong her life, but no one cared to postulate on how long.

As soon as Lia was out of the car, Mariam rushed forward and pulled her sister into her arms. Her face was twisted as she tried to stop her tears, "You don't know how much I have missed you." Her eyes were suddenly blurred as her heart sank. Lia seemed so much smaller then she remembered, and so frail.

Lia returned her sister's hug, while her other arm reached for her mother who had a hard time hiding the shock at seeing her other daughter after so many years. Sarah, embracing Lia and looking to Jarrod, she reached out to clasp his hand. She smiled at him and saw the twinkle in his eyes brighten as they remembered the last time they had met.

"Welcome to the Nunnery," she told him, thinking, He still looks loose-limbed, but not so skinny.

Jarrod was of medium height, with thick, light brown hair and very fine, dark grey eyes. They were darker than his daughter's and his eyebrows were almost black. "Thank you, Sarah," Jarrod said warmly, accepting the hand as a peace offering.

Noting Lia's exhaustion, Sarah told Jarrod, "I'll take her upstairs. She needs to rest for a while."

"Yes, thank you, Sarah."

Sarah led her daughter upstairs, leaving Jarrod and Mariam to deal with the luggage.

Mariam grinned at him, then, more seriously, "Is Lia all right?"

"No. I'm afraid she's failing fast. The last two weeks of the trip, she needed to rest more often; she quickly tires."

"I'm glad she's home."

Sarah led Lia up to her old room and when she opened the door, Lia smiled.

"Yes, Mother, I can see I'm home."

"I left it the way it was when you went away, hoping that someday you would come home again. Now get undressed and lie down."

When Lia came out of the bathroom and lay down, Sarah spread the covers over her and sat down on the bed. "Now, child, tell me how are you?"

They visited for a while, Sarah stayed until Lia had fallen asleep.

* * * *

Lia felt less exhausted as she rose from her nap. Looking into the mirror, her face was still pale, but not as drawn, and she did feel better. Before leaving her room, she put on a light robe and stepped out onto the landing. She could hear voices coming from her mother's sitting-room. Lia knocked and at the same time opened the door. Mariam, her Mother, and Jarrod were having tea.

"Lia, come in and join us," Mariam beckoned to her. "We hoped you would sleep a little longer."

Jarrod rose and putting his arm around her waist, whispered, "You look nicely rested." He led her to the couch. "I'll get your tea," and soon brought her a steaming cup.

"Thank you, dear," Lia told him, carefully taking the teacup. "I feel so much better. It's nice to be home," she said to her mother.

After she was comfortable and sipping her tea, her mother asked, "Now, tell us about Naomi?"

Lia took a slow sip as she looked at her mother. Putting the cup down she answered, "Jarrod and I decided to leave her on Sarpedion since she has only two more semesters left to complete her degree."

"Then you think she's all right?"

"She is functional now and she has taken an interest in her studies again."

"Has she recovered much after Caleb's death?"

"No, Mother, I don't think so."

"It was horrible the way Caleb died. They literally had to cut him out of the car. I thought Naomi would never stop screaming. But when she sank into a stupor, I wished she was still screaming," Mariam said, still feeling a heavy and lingering sadness about Caleb Kamenara's death.

"It was a horrible time for her, poor child. Does she know of your illness?"

"Yes, Mother, we told her."

"I don't know if I would have left her." Mariam muttered more to herself than in conversation, shaking her head.

"But Mariam, she is twenty-five years old. She has to learn to stand on her own feet sometime," Lia replied a little huskily. There was a slight tightening around her eyes. Feeling guilty, Lia imagined reproach in Mariam's voice. "But I agree, now was a poor choice."

"Mariam, Lia is worried about her and so am I," Jarrod told her. "But Naomi is finally studying law again."

"I know, Jarrod, I know, but there is something nagging at me."

"A hunch, maybe?" her mother asked.

"Probably."

"Aw Mariam, you and your hunches."

"Lia," their mother said gently. "They have often paid off."

"I am getting my visa ready, and if you don't mind, I'll go to Sarpedion just to be with her."

"Would you do that?" Lia asked eagerly.

"Yes Lia. Like I said, I'm feeling uneasy about Naomi."

* * * *

Within two months after Lia returned to Novalis, her illness worsened. A message was sent to Naomi, explaining to her about her mother's condition and asking her to come home. Mariam was anxiously waiting for the reply from Naomi. Her visa was ready, but if she left now she might miss her. They waited another month, but still no reply.

Then Lia died.

About a week later, a very strange communiqué came from their Embassy on Sarpedion indicating that Naomi had applied for her passport and given the Ambassador her papers. It said that she would be taking a cruise for a week with a man named Eddan el Halugh, and then planned to go home to Novalis. But she never showed. She seemed to have disappeared.

Mariam, coming home, was barely through the door of her mother's sitting room, when she excitedly asked, "Do you have a letter from Naomi?"

"No but something about her. It's from our Embassy on Sarpedion," she answered and handed Mariam the letter.

Mariam scanned it quickly, but halted at the name Eddan el Halugh. "Eddan el Halugh?" she said. "Isn't that a Madrian name?"

"Yes, and I don't like it. Where's Jarrod?"

"As far as I know, he's presenting his first case in court."

"Any idea when he will be back?"

"No I don't," she said, already going toward the door, then, stopped. "Jarrod mentioned something about staying in town. He is planning to fix up the apartment above his office. I guess it would be easier living there than having to come all the way out here every day. Mother, I'm going back into town. Would you mind calling his secretary to make sure she notifies him that I'm coming?"

"Why so worried?"

"Madrians have peculiar ideas about women."

When Mariam arrived at Jarrod's office, his secretary informed her that a note had been sent into the courtroom.

An hour later, the door opened and Jarrod came in.

"Have you heard from Naomi?" was his first question.

"We heard about Naomi," she replied, and handed him the dispatch.

He stood reading it and then sat down heavily in his chair. "I will have to put in for an emergency visa . . ."

"I will come with you."

The frown on Jarrod's forehead eased, "I'm grateful," he told her as he picked up the phone.

"Give it to me," Mariam told him. It was answered by the Ambassador's aide. "Hello, Tessa, this is Mariam. Where is Ambassador Tenser? It's urgent."

"He has been expecting your call and is still in his office. I will put you through."

"Mariam, this is Saul. I have been in contact with the Embassy in Sarpedion. I surmise you and Jarrod will want to go. You're cleared on the next ship out, which is in three days."

"Thanks, Saul. I will be at your office tomorrow."

After she hung up, she relayed, "We can leave in three days. Saul has been in contact with Sarpedion."

* * * *

Mariam and Jarrod were given passage on a courier ship to Sarpedion.

When the ship landed on the planet, they were met by a courtesy car from the Embassy. At the Embassy, they were immediately ushered into the Ambassador's office.

The Ambassador rose from behind his desk. He appeared to be in his mid-forties. The moment Mariam entered, his suddenly warm, bright smile made him look younger by years. He stepped briskly around his desk with outstretched hands.

"Hello, Mariam. I wish our meeting would be for a more pleasant occasion."

"I know, Alon. May I introduce Jarrod Darbani, Naomi's father. Jarrod this is Alon Aziz."

"I'm very glad to meet you. What do you know about my daughter?"

After Mariam and Jarrod were seated in large, soft-padded chairs, Alon regarded Jarrod with concern, then, said, "I understand how eager you must be to hear about your daughter. She was here some time ago telling me about a cruise she would be taking with an Eddan el Halugh. It was supposed to be just for one week and following that, she was planning to go home to Novalis. She gave me all the necessary papers, so I booked passage for her, but she never came back. Two weeks later the Captain of the cruise ship, Dream Boat, came to me with a curious story. I think you should talk to him."

"Is he in port?"

Alon reached for a brochure and leafed through it. "He should still be on Eubea, according to this schedule. The Port is at Styra, the only stopover of his passenger liner on the island."

"I need to call the airport. Alon, would you mind if I use your phone?"

"No, please."

"She has a habit of making herself at home," Jarrod commented.

Alon Aziz smiled. "Oh, we go back a long way. Mariam used to be Novalis' interstellar ambassador to the Planetary Alliance."

"Ah. All along this trip, I've noticed she knows a lot of very important people."

"Jarrod, we have tickets," Mariam interrupted him. "There's a small plane leaving early tomorrow morning.

"What have you planned in the mean time?" Alon asked Mariam.

"I'm sorry, Alon. I seem to be breezing in and out again. I think Jarrod and I should go to the University and find out all we can about this Eddan el Halugh."

"I think that's a good idea. If I can help, let me know."

"The name of a good hotel would be a beginning," Mariam teased him.

"There are several close to the University. How about having dinner with my wife and me tonight?"

"Jarrod?" Mariam asked.

"So far you have done an excellent job of arranging everything."

"Jarrod, I'm sorry . . ."

"Don't let her kid you; she's not," Alon injected, smiling.

"We would gladly accept," Jarrod told him with a grin.

"Then I will see you tonight, about seven. I have a meeting at this very moment, so please excuse me for now."

* * * *

"Mariam, I called the airport and found an earlier plane leaving for Eubea. It's today at four." Jarrod said, walking through the connecting door."

"Jarrod!" Mariam exclaimed. She had just come out of the bathroom and was in her underwear. "I'm glad I didn't come out in my birthday suit."

Jarrod grinned and turned around. "Comes from being married," he offered as his excuse.

"But not to me," she pointed out as she began dressing. Her statement was spoken in a reasonable tone of voice, but had an added hint of warning.

"Sorry about that. I called Alon and canceled our dinner engagement. Until four, I thought we'd dig up some of the students who knew Naomi." Unruffled by the sudden change in the itinerary, Mariam agreed," That's not a bad idea."

"First, let's go to the Dean's office, then, check at the dorm. Maybe the house-mother has kept track of some of the girls who were living there at the same time as Naomi."

"Sounds good. But if you don't mind, I'd like to finish dressing."

Half an hour later they were sitting in the Dean's office.

"Naomi Atossa? Let me find her records." He searched through his computer.

"Mister Darbani, it states here that she is married to an Eddan el Halugh and he asked that her papers be transferred to the University of Hilo on Eubea. We have a copy of the marriage certificate and an authorization from his wife to send the papers."

"Could we have copies?" Mariam asked him.

"Yes, of course. Is something wrong?"

"That's why we are here, to find out."

"Also, we'd like to find out about this Eddan el Halugh," Jarrod told him.

"Let's see," he said, and turned back to his computer. He keyed into the employee record program and after a few minutes came up with Eddan el Halugh's file. "All I have here is that he worked for the University for a short time, then, quit the job. I only have his address here on Sarpedion and nothing from Madras."

"When did he work here?"

"Five years ago."

Jarrod looked at Miriam. "That was long before he met Naomi."

"I'm sorry, but that's all I have on him."

Their next stop was Naomi's old dorm. They were able to locate the apartment manager. Mariam asked if she remembered Naomi Atossa.

"Naomi Atossa? Let's see." the woman thought for a while. "Ah, yes," she said, "Petite . . . really a wisp of a girl. Nice and friendly, but very quiet. I would say she was withdrawn, kept to herself, rarely joining the other girls. Yes, I remember her. She left all of a sudden during the school break and never returned. What happened to her?"

"That's why we're here." Mariam told her. "We'd like for you to check if there's still someone here who knew her."

"Let me see what I have on my computer." She brought up Naomi's file. "I still have Naomi in my computer. She is listed as coming back, but hasn't. There's only one girl still here who I think knew her, name of Lisa. I'll call and see if she has a moment."

A few minutes later, a knock on the door was followed by the voice and curious face of a young woman.

"Yes, Miss Halla?"

"Come on in, Lisa. This is Mariam Atossa, Naomi's aunt and Jarrod Darbani, Naomi's father. They would like to ask you some questions."

"What kind of questions?"

"We would like to find out what happened to Naomi. Miss Halla tells us that she left here quite suddenly and never came back. What can you remember?"

Lisa's eyebrows rose in slight surprise as she looked at Mariam. "She didn't go home?" Lisa asked, somewhat dismayed.

"No, she never came home."

"Oh, damn," Lisa said. She looked at Mariam, then Jarrod and blushed. "Sorry," she said quickly, then continued. "Naomi wanted to go back to Novalis as soon as the semester was over. She was worried about her mother. I thought she would be all right since she was going to go home."

"Why were you worried about her?"

"Well, Miss Atossa, there was this guy hanging around her. He was a Madrian. Naomi didn't really like him. But he kept coming around. He helped her with her homework, and they went out together. He kept sneaking around her room and going through her mail. When I asked, he always had a plausible explanation. One day," Lisa paused and sighed, "I saw him being followed by an older woman who was pleading with him . . . tugging at his arm. Then he suddenly slapped her across the face. If she hadn't been quick enough to move out of the way, he would have kicked her, too. I was going to tell Naomi about it, but she was already getting ready to return to Novalis, so I figured she would be away from him, and it wouldn't matter. Do you know where she is?"

"We are trying to find her."

"I hope she's all right. She was very quiet and didn't know many people, but we got to know each other a bit. I liked her. After you left," Lisa finished, looking at Jarrod, "she became even more withdrawn."

"Thank you Lisa. You have been a great help," Mariam told her. Then, looking at her watch, "We'd better leave now; we have a plane to catch," she said to Miss Halla.

* * * *

After landing on Eubea, they rode a bus to Styra where the Dream Boat was still docked. Before boarding the bus, Jarrod had made a call and talked briefly to the Captain, identifying himself and describing their mission. When they arrived at the ship, the steward was waiting for them on the quay.

"The Captain is on one of the upper decks. It's cooler there," he explained, as they climbed the stairs. "Captain Dasha, this is Mister Darbani and Miss Atossa."

Captain Dasha had papers strewn across a table with more lying on his lap. When he looked up, there was a slight hesitation, then a shrug of his shoulder. "Forgive me for not rising. Please, do sit down," he said, indicating the deck chairs. Gathering the papers, he laid them aside and asked, "Can I get you something?" and turned to the steward. With a wave of his hand, he said, "Bring some of that new fruit drink, will you please?"

"Mister Darbani, I have all the papers ready." Thumbing through the stack, he pulled out several sheaves. "These are several affidavits," he said, and handed them to Jarrod. "They are from the crew and myself, especially the stewards, attesting to what we observed. I'm sorry; I should have been more alert. Afterward, we all agreed that there was something wrong."

"We appreciate very much you coming forward. Thanks to you, the Ambassador was alerted. Was she under any duress?"

"Not that we could see. But she did seem withdrawn, and Mister Halugh was very solicitous of her welfare. However, what we gathered only in hindsight was that she was being manipulated and kept away from the other passengers. We very seldom saw her by herself. Considering everything I can piece together, I believe she very likely had been drugged. Ah, here is Emil with the drinks," the Captain remarked as the steward approached their chairs.

Emil set the tray of drinks on a small side table and was about to leave when the Captain requested, "Tell Mister Darbani and Miss Atossa what you observed."

"Not very much, but I remember Mister Halugh making sure I saw them together in bed after the wedding. But his wife did not look like a happy bride to me. Not like the brides of the three other couples we had at the time. To me, she behaved strangely and so did Mister Halugh. No one cared for him. He seemed arrogant, while Mrs. Halugh seemed to be confused, like walking in a fog. And what really bothered me . . . here was a young woman, newly married, on a holiday cruise and she was always sleeping."

"Thanks, Emil," the Captain told him. He turned towards Jarrod and Mariam and said, "That's about the gist of it. Do you have any leads?"

"We hope to find her at the University of Hilo. She's supposed to be a law student there."

After Jarrod and Mariam finished with their drinks, they rose. Checking his watch, Jarrod explained to the Captain, "We have another bus to catch. We thank you very much for your help."

"Again, I'm sorry, and I wish you the best of luck."

As they left the ship, Mariam looked back, "Dream Boat? Not a very auspicious epithet in Naomi's case."

Chapter Eleven

Immediately after arriving at Hilo, Mariam and Jarrod took a taxi to the University. Again they had called ahead and at the Law Center, a student was waiting for them outside on the steps.

"The Dean is expecting you," he said immediately.

Even before they were fully in the office, the Dean approached them. "I'm glad you came. Naomi has everything arranged to leave here by tomorrow. She's supposed to come into Hilo tonight, and we have booked a flight for her back to Vasilika. We have arranged for her to come to my office. She should be here in about two hours."

"Then, you don't advise us to go to her?"

"No, Miss Atossa. You would only miss her that way."

"Where does she live?" Jarrod asked.

"As far as I know at a god-forsaken place out in the country. The police are looking for Eddan el Halugh. She reported that he had kidnapped her and stolen her credit cards. Also, she has graduated. I arranged for an oral and she passed."

"I think that's the only good news we have so far concerning her."

"Miss Atossa, I'm sorry. As soon as we learned about her plight, the University staff tried to assist her."

"I was told that it was you who notified the Ambassador."

"Yes and the police had a hard time tracking el Halugh. He actually worked only a few weeks at the University. Any current job was a lie he told Naomi. There's an older woman, a widow, he has been living with. The police are currently watching her house and will arrest him as soon as he shows up. They are also trying to locate a Mrs. Reno, Naomi's housekeeper. The most I can do right now is to give you the widow's address."

Mariam and Jarrod boarded yet another taxi and gave the address to the driver. The neighborhood was middle-class and pleasantly quiet. The house was recessed from the street. A stone pathway led through the small lawn to the covered porch.

"This time, let me do the talking," Jarrod told Mariam. "She might be suspicious if a woman asks after him."

Mariam grinned. "She probably would. Sorry, if I've been monopolizing conversations. I don't mean to."

Jarrod flashed her an amused smile as he rang the doorbell.

A woman in her late fifties opened the wood-paneled door. She wore a white short-sleeved blouse and a long, flowered skirt. Mariam imagined she had been very pretty in her younger days with the large blue eyes and fair skin. But now, any real prettiness had faded.

"Yes, can I help you?" she asked, holding the door only partially open, her eyes narrowed.

Mariam got the impression the woman was more nervous than suspicious.

"We would like to speak to Eddan el Halugh, if possible," Jarrod told her.

"I don't know where he is," she replied hastily, with obvious apprehension.

With a friendly smile and a reassuring tone, Mariam added, "We only want to talk to him."

"He was supposed to come home yesterday, but he never . . ." Her hand flew to her mouth as if she feared she had said too much.

"Miss, our main concern is for a young woman, and we think he could help us," Mariam said.

"A young woman?" the widow asked.

"Do you know something . . . anything at all?" Jarrod asked, hopefully.

"Please." Her alarm seemed to dissipate with Jarrod's anxious tone. "Do come in." She led them into a sunny room with wide windows, allowing a view of a large garden. "Please, sit down."

"Ms . . . ?" Jarrod asked.

"Oh, I'm so sorry to be remiss. I'm Ms. Hanna. A widow. I live here by myself." Suddenly she blushed pink. "Well, I did. I mean . . . I have no relatives and I'm quite alone."

Jarrod hid his smile with difficulty, noticing her discomfiture as they took the offered chairs. "Ms. Hanna, I'm Jarrod Darbani and this is my sister-in-law, Mariam Atossa. We're looking for Eddan who may have knowledge of the whereabouts of my daughter, Naomi."

"Naomi? I don't think I have ever heard him mention that name."

"She's a student at the University of Hilo."

"No, he never mentioned her."

"Have you known Eddan el Halugh a long time?"

"No only for about four months. I met him at the University College President's tea party. My late husband was a professor emeritus, so I'm still invited at times. Eddan seemed such a nice gentleman, well-mannered . . . good listener. I began inviting him here to visit. Then he came more and more often, bringing flowers and little gifts. One day, he told me he was a detective working for the Embassy of Madras, investigating the disappearance of a young woman from there. More recently, he told me that the kidnappers were after him and he had to lie low for a while. That's why I was so worried when you inquired about him . . . that maybe you were the kidnappers looking for him. He also asked if he could stay with me. Naturally, since I'm a widow and alone, I didn't mind. Then he said he had to flee his apartment and was without funds, so I advanced him five hundred Sekels . . ."

"That's quite a lot of money," Mariam injected.

"I agree, but he assured me that as soon as the investigation was over, he would be able to pay me back."

Jarrod felt sorry for having to dissolution her. She was evidently a nice lady, though too trusting. "Ms. Hanna, what I'm about to tell you will come as a shock. You see, Eddan el Halugh never worked for the Embassy, and he has no income. He has been living on my daughter's stipend and her credit cards, which he maxed. The kidnapped young woman is my daughter, and it is he who kidnapped her," Jarrod told her.

At first, Ms. Hanna eyed him dubiously, then her stare widened and she paled. She sat perfectly still for a moment and then tears began to well. She pulled a handkerchief from her skirt pocket and sniffed as she dabbed at her eyes. "Oh dear," she muttered. "Oh dear. How could I have ever been such a fool? Are you sure?"

"Yes, Ms. Hanna," Jarrod told her.

"He really took me in. I thought because he had been invited by the Dean . . . oh dear, what a gullible fool you must think me. There were times when I thought his stories were too good, but he always managed to have a reasonable explanation for everything." Looking at Jarrod, "It was your daughter?"

"Yes. We are trying to retrace his steps to find her."

Suddenly, the door flew open and four men with guns drawn erupted into the room.

"Raise your hands and don't move!"

Mariam's first thoughts were how melodramatic the scene was, but obediently raised her hands into the air.

"Sir," Mariam addressed the senior officer, "if you reach into this gentleman's coat pocket, you will find his identification."

The officer looked at her, then cautiously edged up to Jarrod and reached deftly into his pocket for the wallet.

"Sorry, sir," he said after reading the identification on Jarrod's passport. We are looking for an Eddan el Halugh."

"So are we, and for my niece Naomi Atossa. I'm Mariam Atossa, Interstellar Ambassador of the planet Novalis," she said and handed him her identification.

"We found the house where he was keeping Miss Atossa, but it was already vacated. We had an officer standing guard across from here and he notified us that a man and a woman had entered."

"Oh god, will this nightmare ever end?" Jarrod groaned. "Each time we think we're close, she disappears again. Have you any idea where they have gone?"

"No not yet. We have circulated his and Naomi Atossa's identities to several airports, especially the one here on Eubea. Can I use your phone?" the officer asked Ms. Hanna.

"Yes, of course. But may I sit down?"

He looked at Ms. Hanna and realized she had turned very pale and her hand was shaking as she reached for the back of a chair for support.

"Of course. I'm sorry to have frightened you." He picked up the phone and made several calls.

"A private plane, you said? Oh, a charter plane. What was it's destination? . . . Vasilika? . . . Thanks."

His next call was to Vasilika's space station.

"Has any shuttle arrived at the station or a ship left for Madras?" he asked the tower and switched the phone over to speaker, so the others could listen.

"We cleared a cargo ship for Madras."

"Any passengers?"

"Four. Three men and a woman."

"How long ago?"

"About two hours."

"So they're beyond recall."

"What's going on?"

"We suspect that there is a kidnapped woman on board."

"I don't think they would come back, and we don't have the authorization to recall them. They're beyond our jurisdiction by now."

"Thanks, tower," he said as he abruptly hung up.

He looked at Jarrod. "Sorry, we tried." he said.

"I know," Jarrod told him, running his hand through his hair. "Mariam?"

Mariam had sat back in the chair and was chewing on her thumb. When she looked up, her expression was determined. "This has turned into an interstellar felony. As an interstellar ambassador, I am commandeering an airplane to fly us to Vasilika. Can you assist us?"

"We'll help you all we can. Come with us. I will radio ahead from my car."

Before they left, Ms. Hanna reached out with her hand to Jarrod and said, "I hope you find your daughter."

"Thank you, Ms. Hanna," Jarrod returned as he took the offered hand and gently touched her shoulder.

* * * *

At Vasilika space port, Mariam contacted Novalis' representative to the Planetary Alliance at the Headquarters on the planet Daugave.

After she told him her story, he asked, "What do you want me to do?"

"Get me transportation to Madras. This is a kidnapping. It's an interstellar offense."

"Mariam, I don't know if you can get it. It will involve some military . . . even political tactics. And just how high up are you prepared to go with this?"

"If I don't get any action, I'm prepared to come to Daugave to see Admiral Omi Hireyoshi."

She could hear a short chuckle. "He still remembers you favorably over the negotiations between Madras and Daugave on women's rights. Now . . . I recall you have a well-prepared case for Naomi Atossa?"

"Yes, my niece had contacted every accessible embassy, and I have affidavits from the captain and steward of a pleasure cruiser and several other people at her university."

"I would like to have those documents."

"I will gladly send them to you, but now, how about transportation to Madras?"

"I will arrange for a courier ship.

* * * *

At the Port of Entry on Madras, Mariam and Jarrod were met by the Madrian Ambassador to the Planetary Alliance. Mariam had met him twice before on Daugave, and the meetings had not been cordial. So he now greeted her with a sour smile and stiff mien. "Mariam Atossa, welcome to Madras."

"Thank you Ambassador Karzan for your consideration in meeting us," she said coolly. "May I introduce Jarrod Darbani, my brother-in-law."

Karzan immediately turned to Jarrod. "I understand that you are looking for your daughter."

"Yes sir."

"I have not personally looked into this matter, but inquiries have been made, and information has it that she is the wife of an Eddan el Halugh," he said, still stiff-lipped.

"Mister Ambassador, my niece was kidnapped and drugged. I doubt she gave her consent to this alleged marriage."

His tone became icy as he replied, "That might be. But we have no . . ."

"Ambassador Karzan," Mariam interrupted him, "This is a well-documented case, and I am prepared to contact Admiral Hireyoshi if need be."

The Ambassador glared at Mariam with implacable dislike, deploring what he considered her tactless interruption. "I don't think that will be necessary," he said curtly. His voice had risen in spite of his efforts to maintain a dignified level, so this was listed as an additional demerit against Mariam Atossa.

Jarrod knew it was time to intercede and laid a tempering hand on Mariam's arm as he spoke calmly to Karzan, "We are willing to conduct this affair as quietly as possible. We only ask for your assistance, if needed. Right now, we would like to go to the Planetary Embassy of Novalis."

"I have a car waiting, and will convey you there, myself."

"Thank you, Ambassador Karzan."

At the Embassy of Novalis, they were met by Ambassador Dravian Montoya, another good friend of Mariam, Jarrod noted.

"Mariam my dear, how nice to see you again. Greetings Mister Darbani. Ambassador Karzan, welcome to the Embassy of Novalis." Turning back to Mariam, he continued. "I received your dispatch. Also one from our embassy on Sarpedion. I would also like to have all of your documentation."

"I'm willing to give it to you as soon as we have Naomi safely with us."

"Ambassador Karzan, may I ask your assistance in this?"

"We have already looked into this matter and will give you what we have so far."

"We would like to study all the information you have on the el Halugh family."

"That, I will send over tomorrow. I wish you a good evening and hope this will be resolved to your satisfaction." He bowed to Montoya, and with the diplomatic smile fixed upon his lips as if painted there, gave Jarrod a slight bow and a curt nod to Mariam before he was escorted out of the Embassy.

To Montoya's amusement, Mariam quipped, "I never liked him."

"So you spar with him?"

"I don't like his arrogance. We have clashed the proverbial sword before. He would like for me to be compliant to his superiority."

Montoya still smiled at her. "What you really don't like is his sexist attitude," he teased her.

"You're right about that."

"Have you eaten yet?"

"No, but that's not what made me grumpy." Turning to Jarrod, "We better leave now before Dravian and I start a long discussion, considering we still have to find some sort of accommodations." Mariam's true desire at that moment was to avoid further discussion about Karzan, whom she had long despised.

"You could stay at my residence."

"Your offer is very generous, Dravian, but we'll settle for a hotel and see you tomorrow at your convenience to get this matter moving. Thank you for your graciousness." The three shook hands goodnight.

They were riding in a chauffeured limousine when Jarrod, using the car phone, finished making a hotel reservation, then said to Mariam, "You were somewhat short with Ambassador Montoya."

"Jarrod, my dear, I don't take advantage of friends. Besides, it was kind enough of him to have us chauffeured to our hotel."

I guess I've been told off, Jarrod thought. Leaning back in the seat, he studied her profile. She was a remarkable woman and probably equally exasperating to live with as he had gathered from

Dravian's remarks. In many ways, she reminded him of Lia. But where Lia had been a steady and strong current running through his life, Mariam was more like quicksilver and seemed seldom to relax. His relationship with Lia had been a difficult one in the beginning, but despite the few years it took, they had reached a wonderful compatible stage. Lia, like Mariam, had been very independent.

What am I contemplating? he wondered and brought himself up short. Then he smiled in spite of himself. The marriage with Lia had proven a memorable one. Maybe? he thought, possible?, . . . his brow rising slightly.

* * * *

The phone rang in the middle of the night, and Mariam groped for the instrument. "Yes," she said.

"Mariam, this is Dravian. Come to my house. I'll send a car."

"All right," Mariam mumbled and hung it up, promptly falling back to sleep, having never fully awakened.

"Mariam!"

Someone was shaking her. She huffed and opened her eyes.

"Jarrod! What are you doing in here?"

"What was the phone call about?"

"What phone call?"

"The phone just rang and you answered it."

"I did?"

"Mariam, wake up!"

Mariam sat up and looked at Jarrod. "You know this could be misconstrued, you being in my bedroom, especially on Madras. What time is it?"

"About five in the morning."

Suddenly she let out a yelp. "God, Dravian called! Get dressed; he's sending a car." When they reached the bottom of the stairs, a young man was stepping through the glass doors. "I think we are your fare," Mariam told him.

"Yes, I think so. Mister Montoya sent me."

At Montoya's residence, they drove into his underground garage. Dravian stood there waiting for them.

"Good morning, Mister Darbani. Did you have some difficulty waking her?"

"You seem to know her well. And, please, call me Jarrod."

"We once had to pretend to be husband and wife."

"Oh, I see. That explains it."

"Come upstairs. I have a visitor."

In the middle of the Ambassador's living room was someone obviously very ill at ease and pacing.

"This gentleman came to me tonight, and I want you to listen to him."

The stranger turned to Jarrod. "I won't be telling you my name or any name involved in this," he said. "Tomorrow, precisely at nine o'clock be at the junction of the Roy el Bashir Avenue and High Road. There will be a grey sedan. Naomi will be driving. You will need to leave Madras immediately. I wish you luck."

He bowed and with long strides left.

"Now that I have managed to close my mouth," Mariam said, "can you elaborate?"

"No, I don't know who he is. I met him only once before when I was given some rigmarole about Naomi and told to be on standby until further notice. I guess Naomi has friends. Or, just someone who wants her out of the way for reasons of their own."

"Then you think this is legit?" Jarrod asked.

Dravian harrumphed sharply and scratched his head as he looked at Jarrod. "Mariam knows that the Madrians are very good at intrigue. But I would take this on face value and be there at nine in the morning."

"Is the courier ship still in port?"

For a moment Dravian gazed thoughtfully at Mariam. He was attuned to the quick way her mind worked. "I can ascertain that," he told her, unruffled.

There were several conversations that night with persons on Daugave and Novalis. About seven-thirty in the morning, Dravian, exhausted and bleary eyed, put the phone down and turned to Mariam who was by now sound asleep.

"I don't know how she does it. She can sleep anywhere or anytime," he told Jarrod who sat tired and red-eyed in his chair.

"Mariam, wake up," he said, shaking her shoulders.

Mariam came instantly awake. "Dravian, you have some nerve, rousing me out of a good dream," she chided him and stretched. "What have you found out?"

"The courier ship is still in port, but it has been requisitioned to the Altair System. However, it can intersect with a starship patrolling between the planets Daugave and Khitan, and it can easily divert its course to Novalis. I have established a beam-over point."

"Great job, Dravian," Mariam said with a broad smile, patting his back and giving him a peck on the cheek. "Now, how do we leave your house unseen?"

"Before my butler comes in. He's a Madrian, and as you know, they like to gossip, or more importantly, sell information."

But it was too late. The door opened; the butler had arrived a bit early. He paused for a split second in surprise, then asked unperturbed, "Mister Montoya, would you like to have breakfast served in the dining room?"

"Yes, please, and also for my guests."

As soon as Jarrod and Mariam had gone, Dravian went to his office and called his secretary to come in.

"I need to borrow your car," he stated as evenly as if asking for a cup of tea.

"Of course, sir," his secretary agreed quickly, but wondered at the unusual request.

"I need you to go to the Savoy. There are two friends of mine staying there. I want you to let them have your car. One is a red-haired wom . . ."

"Mariam Atossa?" he secretary injected quickly.

"Yes. But you won't remember anything about this. Take a taxi back here to the Embassy, and we'll pick up your car later.

* * * *

After sharing the Ambassador's breakfast, Jarrod and Mariam had taken a taxi back to their hotel and hurriedly packed. It would be a forty-five minute drive to get to the junction of Roy el Bashir Avenue and the High Road.

Chapter Twelve

Hadjar was sitting up in his bed, studying the young girl still sleeping bedside him. If she has a little more spunk, I might just keep her, he thought. Maybe I will make her a consort, or even another wife? He chuckled softly in his throat. Wonder how Saada would like it, the whey-faced bitch. I never know how I stand with her. Only to himself did he acknowledge that she was much smarter than he. She was good at bookkeeping and would be nearly impossible to replace. The thought annoyed him so much he scowled down at the girl, then, hit her on the butt.

Still half asleep, she wheeled to face him. "Why did you do that?" she demanded. "I was good last night."

"Yes, Lessa, you were good last night, but this is today. Now get up and get my breakfast."

She grumbled, but left the bed.

"If you're not nice, I will tumble you one more time," Hadjar threatened her."

She swiveled around and moved her body sensuously as she came toward him. "Would you?" she asked with a saucy grin on her face.

"Uh, get out of here and get me my breakfast." He relaxed against his pillows. I'm getting too old for this, he thought, as he watched the door close behind her.

A short while later there was a knock on his door and Boufaric entered the room. "You said you wanted to look at that filly this morning?"

"Yes, after I have had my breakfast. Did Sidi come down on his price?"

"Nope, but she will make a good mare, and he knows she's worth what he's asking. Saada called. She wants someone to pick her up."

"She's yearning to see me?"

This amused Boufaric and he smiled. "It's more like having to get the papers ready to pay the taxes. I think they're due the first of next month."

"Send Naomi. By the way, how is she doing?"

"As far as I know, she's fine. She was helping Mari with the garden and canning."

"And my precious Eddan?"

"He hasn't been home."

"Still with that swing group?" Hadjar asked, and then roared with laughter. He knew his offsprings and didn't begrudge their time for a little distraction.

Boufaric simply chuckled.

"Now how about you?"

Boufaric swallowed and turned red in the face. "I'm not much for swinging," he told his father. "I don't mind a tumble now and then, but all that is not my scene."

"I know that, you fool. I want to know when you're going to get yourself a wife."

To Boufaric's relief, the door open and Lessa came in with the breakfast tray. "I'll see you downstairs," Boufaric told him.

Outside the room, he expelled a full chest of air. That damned fool doesn't get it. Who would want their daughter to marry into this family? he mused. Walking down the hallway, Boufaric came across Moshja. "What are you doing here?" he asked the boy. "Are you finished saddling the horses?"

Moshja scowled. "Yes, Boufaric, they're saddled. I just came in to tell you."

Yeah, sure, Boufaric thought, knowing it to be a lie. Probably was on his way to the kitchen to see what he can snatch. Moshja was one of Hadjar's offsprings by one of the consorts. There were several other such children running around the place. He didn't mind, but Saada might be another matter. The majority had been born after she had married Hadjar.

"Tell Naomi to pick up Saada, and tell her to be prompt."

"Why does she always get to drive the car into town?" Moshja grumbled.

"When you are old enough to drive, it might become your job."

"Hah! Used to, Mari would take me along, but now it's always Naomi."

"Quit bitching and go about your business," Boufaric told him. Following behind to oversee his order, he heard Moshja relaying the message.

"Can't it wait?" Naomi asked. "I need to get this basket to the wash house and start the laundry . . ."

"No, you don't," Boufaric cut in."

"What's the hurry?"

"Saada still has to get the taxes ready. They are due soon," Boufaric explained, coming up beside her. "She wanted to come in last night, but was delayed."

"All right," Naomi said, giving Moshja the basket.

Boufaric looked at Moshja who stood, still staring after Naomi. "What's keeping you?" he asked harshly.

"All right, I'm going. Quit biting my head off."

"Insolent brat," Boufaric mumbled, but with some tolerance. He didn't mind Moshja. But if Hadjar thought he'd liked the boy, he would just play one against the another.

So far, everything he and Sidi had planned had gone according to schedule. Hopefully, Naomi doesn't take her time driving into Sikar, he thought.

"Naomi," he heard Mari shout, "Saada just called to say hurry up."

"I'm on my way," Naomi called back. She quickly went to get her purse before heading to the garage.

"Good," Boufaric thought, relieved.

Tomorrow night one of Sidi's friends would be taking Eddan to a party in town. There would be a good number of females, and Sidi would instruct the caterer to ensure there were plenty of oysters on the menu. They wanted Eddan to be sick and out of the way for a couple of days.

Two weeks ago, Sidi had gone to the Embassy of Novalis as Naomi had asked him. Upon his return, he informed Boufaric that Naomi's father and aunt were expected at the Embassy, that their ship would be arriving soon.

After Hadjar had pressed Eddan to produce an offspring, Saada had hinted to Boufaric that it would not be a good idea for Hadjar to have a grandson. Naomi would just become another pawn for him to play with. A smirk crept across Boufaric's face. In her indirect way, his mother was the schemer of much that went on by way of hint dropping. When he was a young boy, Saada had told him never to show fear, no matter how mean and outrageous Hadjar was. But more than her words had been her own deportment and her placid acceptance of everything Hadjar dished out, never showing her true feelings. She always did as Hadjar asked. Boufaric had learned to read his mother's cues. Some time ago, in just that way, she had conveyed her intent to help Naomi escape. He had overheard their conversation that afternoon on the hill and he had put the pieces together. Saada had her own agenda. She was still young, and she was patient.

"Boufaric," Hadjar bellowed. "What are you doing standing there like a dumb ass? What are you sulking about? I want you to think about what we discussed. I want you to find a wife. It's about time you had kids."

Boufaric felt a jolt. He could not afford getting Hadjar cross, or he might cancel the trip to Sidi el Asnam's estate. "Yes, Father, I'm thinking about it all the time," he assured Hadjar with a broad grin. "What I was just now thinking about is this filly. If we bred her to the black stallion, since he is so long-legged, it would add speed to the foal. Don't you think?"

"You're way too preoccupied with horses," Hadjar grumbled, but his peevishness evaporated. He liked this son, but it would do no good to show it. He wanted to keep Boufaric off balance. It was why he had been so adamant that Eddan produce a child. Need to find out if it is a boy . . . ought to get rid of it, no matter what it is, he considered. I don't want any offspring from that bloodless idiot of a son. Aw, Saada, if you weren't so indispensable. Maybe

I should have Naomi study bookkeeping . . . hmm.
Seriously, it wouldn't be such a bad idea. The thought
lightened his mood as he mounted his horse. It
suddenly amused him so much, he chuckled. It would
serve Saada right. He turned his horse and rode off
toward the el Asnam Estate with Boufaric falling in
beside him.

* * * *

Naomi was driving on the highway, relieved to be
for a time away from Oran. She was always on pins
and needles, trying to make herself as inconspicuous
as possible . . . especially when Hadjar was around.
She was not as frightened now as she had been; she
was seeing very little of Eddan lately. The only one
with whom she felt somewhat at ease was Mari. What
a strange household with so many undercurrents. Why
would Saada want to come home all of a sudden? The
tax papers are just an excuse for what?

It was close to nine when she turned onto Roy
el Bashir Avenue. Damned traffic jam! She inched
along until she had reached the High Road junction.
At the intersection a car had lost control and stopped
the flow of traffic. Naomi was just turning the corner
onto High Road, when someone rapped on the
opposite window. Startled, she was about to scream

when her father's face stared in at her. She rolled down the window, and he shouted, "Naomi, find a place to park."

"Father?" Taking her hands off the steering wheel, Naomi froze for a second, thinking her senses were playing tricks on her, but then she watched as he reached in and opened the door.

"Hurry," he said his voice urgent, as he dropped into the seat beside her.

Her mouth was dry. She was shaking as she drove into the parking lot of the nearby mall. As she parked the sedan, she grabbed her purse when she noticed another car stopped beside hers. Her father was grabbing her by the hand on her side of the sedan, pulling her out. He shoved her into the back seat of the other car.

"Aunt Mariam!"

"Get on the floor and keep your head down."

"What's going on?" Naomi asked.

"Can't you see you are being rescued, young lady," her Father whispered.

Naomi's gaze went from her father to her aunt. "How did you find me?" she asked, her lips quivering as she tried not to cry.

"You left enough clues, dear," her aunt told her as she drove toward the exit. "What happened at Eubea?"

"What do you mean?"

"The police went to the little house in the woods, but you were gone."

"Oh, God," Naomi said and shuddered. "Eddan's brother and a cousin came and made us go with them. We left for Madras in a freighter."

"Well, keep low, until we board the ship," Mariam told her as she eased the car into traffic.

"Ship, what ship?"

"A spaceship, Naomi, a spaceship," Jarrod told her.

Naomi curled up on the floor and Jarrod looking over the front seat could see the tightly clenched fists and knew she was praying.

* * * *

"Sidi, you're a rogue," Hadjar bellowed, and clapped him on the shoulder.

"Hadjar, it's no use to dicker with me. I know a good horse when I see one, just like you do. She's worth every Sekel," Sidi told him, and laughed while he stroked the horse's rump.

"Boufaric, what do you say?"

"Father, I tried to haggle him down, but as you can see, he's stubborn."

He and Sidi had been friends since school days. Boufaric had spent as much time as he had been allowed on the Asnam Estates. Early on, he had noticed the difference between Sidi's family and his own. As a little boy, he had often wished his father were more like Sidi's.

"You've been woolgathering all day." Hadjar broke into Boufaric's reverie. "Sorry, I was thinking about the bay mare," he prevaricated. "She's about due to foal. Last year she had a hard time, and we had to call in the vet. When we're finished here, I think I'll go and check on her."

"Why don't you? Sidi and I can finish up here," Hadjar told him."

"If you don't mind I think it would be a good idea," Boufaric said. He swiftly rode away, trying to put as much distance between himself and his father whose company he could never stomach for long.

I hope the plan works, Boufaric thought as he relaxed in the saddle.

Last week, he and Sidi had been at the race track in Sikar. While there, he had been introduced to the Ambassador of Novalis from whom he learned the day and time that Naomi's father was expected to land on Madras. Four days before the ship landed, Saada was to make an appointment with her doctor. She had already being complaining about her back. Also, her extra long stay with her sister in order to help out was worked into their plot.

The cue that everything was in place had been for Sidi to call and ask

Hadjar if he was still interested in the mare, hinting that he had another buyer. Then, before Hadjar and Boufaric left for the el Asnam Estate, someone called for Naomi to pick up Saada. The script went perfectly: her sisters company had left and she wanted to come home, and she still had the taxes to do.

Hadjar was now out of the house and probably would stay away for a day or more. He would be gone with Sidi's father at a horse auction in the next town which they frequented. And most likely they would celebrate the buy of the horse since it would be a good bargain for them both.

* * * *

Two days later Hadjar returned home, setting the whole household into an uproar. He strode through the rooms, pretending that nothing pleased him. It took a while for him to notice that Saada wasn't home.

"Mari!" he bellowed, "Where's Saada?"

"She's in Sikar, staying with her sister."

"I thought she was in a hurry to come home. She was griping about needing to do the taxes."

"I will call her."

Mari went to the phone and made the call.

"Well, what did she say?" he barked when she finished the call.

"Azena is still having guests, and Saada decided to stay a little longer and help."

"Give me the phone. Saada, where is the grey sedan?"

"I don't have it."

"Mari said you called for the car to pick you up. You wanted to come home to do the taxes."

"Hadjar, dear, I never called. My sister had guests coming . . ."

"I know all that. Where's Naomi and Eddan?"

"I haven't seen either of them. Ask Mari."

"Mari said that Naomi went to pick you up."

"But Hadjar, I never called to be picked up."

"Boufaric!" Hadjar bellowed. When he didn't appear immediately, he added some choice words to his son's name and then, "Boufaric, where's Eddan?" His face was becoming alarmingly suffused with color.

"Eddan? How should I know," Boufaric answered, as he strolled into the room and shrugged.

"I want him found."

"I could go into . . ."

"I'll go," Hadjar interrupted him curtly, and slammed the phone down.

Saada met Hadjar on the steps of her sister's house. She greeted him as calmly as she could. "Hadjar, you look upset."

"I am. I want to know what this tom foolery is all about. No one seems to know where Eddan or Naomi is," Hadjar demanded heatedly.

"Maybe they wanted to be together for a while and went to visit some of Eddan's friends. I'm sure Eddan will turn up sooner or later," Saada placated.

The more time passes before Eddan is found, the better, Saada thought. She had no idea what had happened to Naomi while she was en route to Sikar. From there Naomi ceased to be her problem. But Eddan still was. He was supposed to be at a friend's place, sleeping off a drinking spree and orgy. She knew all about Eddan's debaucheries, and she guessed so did Hadjar.

"Come on in," Saada coaxed. "Amir will be glad to see you. He is still at breakfast. Have you eaten?"

Hadjar grumbled, but complied, taking the steps two at a time. Azena came to meet him inside the door.

"Welcome, Hadjar," she said pleasantly, "Amir is still having breakfast. Would like to join him?"

"Good morning, Azena," Hadjar greeted her courteously. He exchanged a few polite but meaningless pleasantries, while following her to the breakfast room.

Amir was the antithesis of Hadjar. Where Hadjar was wiry, Amir was stout. He and his slender wife were both congenial people who enjoyed life and family. When Hadjar entered, Amir rose. "Good morning, Hadjar." Pointing to an empty chair, he suggested, "Why don't you sit down; there's still plenty of food. And if you want something special, Azena will gladly get it for you."

"Good morning, Amir." Hadjar responded politely and took the chair offered. Saada immediately began serving him.

In the beginning, Hadjar had thought of Amir as negligible. He always seemed jovial and good-natured. But it slowly dawned on him that Amir was an astute business man and well-educated.

"What brings you to town?" Amir asked, hiding his surprise. He had no idea why Hadjar would call on him so early. As a rule, they both refrained from visiting each other's houses.

"I seemed to have misplaced a son and his wife. No one knows where they are," he said. When he looked at Saada, his face darkened and his eyes narrowed, trying to read her expression. But as always, her face was bland and registered no emotion. It wasn't the first time he wondered what went on behind her seemingly unruffled moon face. He turned to Amir, "Have you seen Eddan or Naomi?"

"No, but then Eddan has been known to disappear for considerable lengths of time. He will turn up again, as he always does." Amir dismissed it with a slight wave of his hand.

"The sedan is also missing. There was a call from Saada wanting Naomi to pick her up, but as it turns out, Saada never made any such call."

"Who took the call?" Saada asked.

"According to Mari, it was Lila, one of the consorts."

"And she said I called?"

"We could call the police," Amir suggested. "There is always a possibility of foul play."

"Fearing something like that is why I came into town."

"Let me make the call. I know the police commissioner."

Amir made the call and thirty minutes later, Rashid el Kasim, a long-standing friend of the family, was shown into Amir's study by Saada.

Amir and Hadjar both rose from the comfortable leather chairs where they had been reclining, discussing possible explanations.

"Good morning, Amir," Kasim said briskly. "What can I do for you?"

"Good morning Rashid. Thank you for responding so soon. May I introduce Hadjar el Halugh, my brother-in-law."

At the mention of the Halugh name, Rashid el Kasim's friendly smile turned a few degrees cooler. Rashid el Kasim sat down in the large leather-padded recliner indicated by Amir, while Saada went to stand behind Hadjar.

The el Halugh reputation was well known, and Rashid was aware of suspicions about Hadjar's second wife, which the police had never been able to prove. His son Eddan was perceived as a wastrel. Since his return to Madras, Eddan had been several times retrieved from houses of ill repute, riotous and drunk.

"What can I do for you, Mister el Halugh?"

"I seem to have misplaced a son and his wife, who is three months pregnant. Also, my grey sedan is missing. As far as I know, they have been gone for three days now. My concern is for Naomi, my son's wife. As I said, she is three months pregnant. There was a call to Oran for Naomi to pick up Saada, my wife. But she says she never made that call. Naomi left Oran for Sikar and she has not been heard from since."

"Could she be with your son, perhaps the two visiting friends, or shopping in town?"

"I think Naomi would have called," Hadjar said. "She is very reliable. She would have let us know where she was, unless something has happened." Hadjar's greatest worry was that Eddan had done something stupid, or maybe absconded, going back to Sarpedion.

Rashid el Kasim turned to Saada. "Could you shed some light on this matter?"

"No sir. As my husband said, Naomi is very reliable. If able, she would have called."

"You did not make that call?"

"No sir. My sister and her husband were expecting guests. Azena asked if I would remain a few days longer to help."

Hadjar looked at Saada. "You were not worried about doing the taxes?"

"Of course not. They are not due for another month. I only mentioned that I would like to do them as soon as possible."

"Did you see your physician?"

Saada hid her smile. He had checked up on her. Meekly she replied, "Yes, Hadjar."

"What did he say?"

"He prescribed hot sit-baths, and some exercises."

"Humph," Hadjar said. "Why don't you go and join Azena. We will talk this over and see what we come up with."

Saada politely inclined her head before retreating.

"Now we need a description of the car, as well as of your son Eddan and his wife. Would he have taken her to any of his usual haunts?"

Hadjar responded rather too quickly and curtly. "No, I think not."

Chapter Thirteen

The gray sedan was found that very day, abandoned at the shopping mall. The mall security had reported the car parked there for several days. The car was gone over thoroughly and checked for finger prints. It revealed nothing unusual.

A day later, an anonymous phone call came to the police about an objectionable odor coming from an apartment. When the police arrived, they had to break down the door, and in the bedroom they found a naked body, male. A very uncomfortable constable was standing guard outside the apartment to open the door when the coroner arrived. "The body is in the bedroom," he told him.

Even before entering the apartment he recognized the smell. "Nasty job; guess he's been dead for some time." The coroner walked through the apartment into the bedroom, and immediately went to the bed and bent over the body. "Hmm, what have we here?" he said to the sergeant standing beside the bed, apparently unmoved by the appalling stench.

The corpse's face was puffy and the lips were pulled back from the teeth. The knees were pulled up to the abdomen, while the hands still clutched the sheets.

Must have been a very painful death, the coroner thought to himself.

The sergeant watched as the coroner made a superficial inspection of the body and asked, "What do you think was the cause of death? There are no marks or injuries I can see."

"Well, I'll tell you after I've done a postmortem. You have his name?"

"It's an Eddan el Halugh. There's a missing person report filed on him and his wife. But he's the only corpse here."

The door opened again and the forensic team arrived. At their heels came Rashid el Kasim. The sergeant stood aside to let him in.

"Are you sure it's Eddan el Halugh?" he inquired, as he entered the bedroom. "Phew, what a stench!"

"He's likely been dead for several days," the coroner explained.

"Here is his identification," the sergeant said, handing him a billfold.

"No obvious cause?"

"No, nothing obvious. But it could be poisoning. Like I said, I will know more after the autopsy."

"Any idea what happened to his wife?" he asked the Sergeant.

"No. His is the only body here."

"Has the family been notified?"

"We're in the process of doing that, sir," the sergeant told him.

"Inform me as soon as you know something. Who is handling the case?"

"Inspector Bakkar, sir. He has gone to the Amir el Asad residence. Hadjar el Halugh and his wife are staying there."

* * * *

Inspector Bakkar walked toward the house. It stood facing the open park with its numerous flower beds and enormous shade trees. It was in the middle of the afternoon, and the sun was scorching. Before he could knock on the door, it was opened by a servant. "I'm Inspector Bakkar, police. May I speak with Amir el Asad?"

"Please, come in. I will inform his lordship."

Bakkar was left standing in the hallway. The house was larger than it had appeared from the outside. He admired the wide staircase leading to a landing, and near him he noted a large potted plant standing underneath the skylight.

When the servant returned, Bakkar was shown into what was clearly a room solely maintained for visitors. It took five minutes before Amir el Asad appeared.

"Good afternoon, Inspector Bakkar. What can I do for you?"

"Good afternoon. I'm sorry to disturb you my lord, but you asked that we report to you if we found Eddan el Halugh."

"And you found him?"

"Yes sir. He's dead."

Asad stared, but quickly recovered from the initial alarm, then asked, "And his wife! Naomi?"

"We only found Eddan el Halugh."

"Hadjar el Halugh isn't here right now. I can give you the address where he can be reached."

"Thank you, Lord el Asad. That would be helpful."

* * * *

Amir went into his study and stood pensively at the window, pressing his palm against his brow. Hadjar had left much earlier to see a friend and Saada was somewhere in the house with Azena. "Hmm." he wondered, why Eddan and not Naomi?" Amir went to pull the bell, and when the servant came in, he said, "Ask Lady Saada to see me in here."

After the servant exited, Amir began to pace. In all the years he had learned not to be surprised by anything Saada did. She was secretive and veiled her feelings. He had asked Azena how Saada felt about Naomi and her pregnancy. He was assured that Saada was not worried about it. This seemed strange to Amir who knew Boufaric was regarded as Hadjar's heir. A male child from Eddan, who was the oldest son, would supplant Boufaric. From infant to adult was a long span of time. Plenty could happen, but still, why would Saada be unconcerned?

Saada knocked on the door, then, stood in the threshold as she let the door swing open. Without entering, she asked, "Amir, you wished to see me?"

"Yes Saada, please come in."

Amir walked to the group of easy chairs near the window and sat down. He motioned for Saada to sit opposite him. When he looked into her face, it was smooth and placid, telling him nothing. "Saada, I have sad news. They found Eddan . . . and he is dead." There was a slight widening of her eyes and Amir thought, Well, this is news to her, too.

"Does Hadjar know?" was her quick response.

"No. As you know, he went this morning to meet with a few friends. He hasn't returned. Or has he?"

"No. What about, Naomi?"

"She wasn't with Eddan. The police still haven't found her. We need to plan how to inform Hadjar. How will he take this news?"

"I don't know," Saada said, almost in a whisper. This was more than she had hoped for. "We were all very surprised when he called Eddan home from Sarpedion. There has never been any love lost between them," she said, her voice growing quieter, and she began to look at her hands in her lap.

"I gathered that. And Naomi?"

"Yes, Naomi. That will be different. She is pregnant and that is important to Hadjar. His hope is for a grandson."

Suddenly, the door burst open and Hadjar strode in. "What is this I hear?" he bellowed at Saada, then, froze when he noticed Amir.

Saada quickly rose from her chair.

Amir could see her swallowing hard, but saying nothing.

"I am sorry, Amir," Hadjar apologized. "The police inform me about Eddan. He is dead. They have no idea where Naomi is. Where is she?" he hurled at Saada, expecting her to give an answer.

Amir answered somewhat icily, "The police haven't found her yet." He looked at Hadjar with dislike, recalling the few times they had met. He had noted a calculated viciousness in Hadjar that always repelled him.

Saada sat down, trying to compose her face, making it as expressionless as possible. She was feeling curiously weak and frightened as she looked into Hadjar's face, trying to read it.

"Can I use your telephone?" Hadjar asked.

"Of course, Hadjar," Amir told him.

He placed a call to Oran. When Moshja answered, he barked "Get me Boufaric or Mari."

"Boufaric is out on the stud farm and . . . Lila, get Mari! Tell her that Lord Hadjar is on the phone!"

Mari came reluctantly to the phone, knowing it was Hadjar. "This is Mari. What can I do for you?" she said politely.

"Have you heard from Naomi?"

"No, Hadjar, and neither have we seen Eddan."

"Eddan is dead," Hadjar said bluntly. "If you hear anything from Naomi, find me immediately."

"Yes Hadjar of course."

* * * *

The coroner opened the inquest on the remains of Eddan el Halugh. He noted that the body had been found under extraordinary circumstances in an apartment Eddan el Halugh had rented the previous month. According to the first doctor at the scene, the man had been dead for several days and likely had died an agonizing death. Also, the death was likely due to poisoning, but the agent causing his death had not yet been identified. The sheets with vomit had been sent to the lab to be analyzed, along with the contents of the stomach.

During the autopsy, it was found that shortly before he died, he had had a full meal that was partly digested. His meal had consisted mostly of crustaceans and mollusks. More lab tests were ordered. Inspector Bakkar reported that he had found evidence in the apartment of a party, so the caterers had been located and the menu obtained. It verified the lab's findings. When asked about his wife, Naomi, Inspector Bakkar reported that he had found no evidence that Naomi el Halugh had ever lived in the apartment. When he showed her picture to neighbors, all of them verified they had never seen her. The inquest was postponed, but the search for Naomi el Halugh continued.

* * * *

"Look here, Naomi has to be somewhere!" Hadjar shouted, and pounded his fist on his desk.

"Hadjar please, shouting at me won't solve anything," Saada pleaded with him.

Everyone steered clear of Hadjar. They avoided any chance of dealing with him while he was in one of his black moods. Saada had reluctantly gone into his office; she needed him to sign the tax forms.

"Did she slip away from someone?"

"I don't think so, Hadjar. We watched her very closely. Pia even went with her into the restrooms downtown. She was never out of anyone's sight when she was in Sikar."

"And when she went to pick you up?"

"I wouldn't know about that. Then she didn't know anyone in Sikar but family."

Hadjar signed the tax forms and silently handed them back to her. Saada quickly left and sighed with relief as she leaned against the wall by the door she had closed softly behind her.

"Is he still angry?" Mari whispered, coming up beside her.

"Yes, nothing has changed."

"He's been in this black mood ever since Eddan's funeral."

"Naomi's disappearance is eating at him."

Mari rolled her eyes to the ceiling and sighed loudly as she walked toward the kitchen.

The last time Saada had spoken to Mari about anything, she had told her to forget everything they had decided about Naomi. Faithfully, Mari did as Saada told her. But it was like walking on a razor's edge where a tiny slip could be disastrous. Hadjar's vengeance would be a terrible one.

* * * *

One of the lab technicians, bending over the spectrograph, turned to the coroner and said, "There's something funny here. Look at it and tell me what you make of it?"

They both were still running the analysis, when Inspector Bakkar walked in.

"Found anything yet?"

"Yes a very curious reading. It shows a synthetic preparation in this food. But for the life of me I can't figure out why it would be there. It interacted adversely with the food he ingested. But then, it should have affected the other people as well."

"Well, what was it?"

"We've never run across anything like it, at least not on Madras."

"Then you don't think . . ."

"That it was murder? If the other people hadn't eaten the same food, yes, I would agree. But no one else suffered any ill effects."

"Then what did he die of?"

"If he had food allergies . . . perhaps. You need to ask the father."

"Hadjar el Halugh will never admit that there was anything wrong with any of his offspring."

"Well, Bakkar, you will just have to step into the lion's den."

* * * *

When Inspector Bakkar arrived at Oran, he was told that Hadjar el Halugh was visiting one of the outlying farms, but that the Lady Saada was at home.

Good, Bakkar thought. I didn't want to talk to el Halugh anyway.

He was ushered into Saada's office on the west side of the main house. It was spacious; one end of the wall was covered by shelves that held hundreds of books. She rose from behind her desk when he walked in.

"Lady Saada, I apologize. I know you're busy, but I need to ask you a few questions, if I may?"

"Yes, of course, if I can help you." She indicated the couch against the wall where several chairs were grouped around a small table. "I think we will be more comfortable there," she told him. Once seated she asked, "What questions do you have?"

Sitting back in the cushions, Bakkar studied her. She was stout, but not overly fat, and her voice was as expressionless as her face.

"Lady Saada, I'm sorry to be troubling you, but I need to know whether Eddan el Halugh had any food allergies?"

Saada did not reply immediately, but frowned, looking at her hands in her lap. She bit her lip, when she looked up. "Inspector Bakkar, I think I need to correct a misconception. Eddan was not my son. When I joined Hadjar el Halugh's household, Eddan was already a grown man, and shortly thereafter left Madras for Sarpedion. I had very little contact with him while he lived here. If he had any food allergies, I am not aware of it."

"Would your husband know?"

"Most likely."

"What was Eddan el Halugh's relationship with his father?"

"Somewhat strained," Saada said dryly. If she had said anything else, Bakkar soon would have discovered the prevarication.

The inspector looked at Saada quizzically. "And his wife, Naomi?"

"Naomi is important to him, because she is going to have his first grandchild."

"And no one has heard from her?"

"No."

"Does she have family?"

"Naomi is from Novalis."

"Oh!" His response was terse. No one has said anything about that. A flash of anger crossed his face. Damn the Madrian's reticence to speak about their women. This put an entirely new angle on her disappearance. "Do you think she has gone back home?"

"Inspector Bakkar, we could speculate from now on and might never reach a conclusion,"

Bakkar smiled slightly, but Saada remained grave when he said, "I stand corrected."

Bakkar's next stop was the Embassy of Novalis. He had made a call from his car, so when he arrived, he was immediately ushered into the Ambassador's office.

"Ambassador Montoya, I'm Inspector Bakkar. Thank you for receiving me so promptly."

Montoya rose from behind his desk and offered his hand. "Inspector Bakkar, please be seated. I was informed that your visit was urgent. How can help you?"

"I'm sorry if I'm imposing, but it's urgent. We are looking for a Naomi el Halugh. We were not aware that she was from Novalis, of the Omicron V System. Her maiden name was Atossa. I hope you have read about the disappearance of Eddan el Halugh and that he was subsequently found dead in his apartment; also of the disappearance of his wife, Naomi. She is three months pregnant."

Montoya looked very grave as he leaned forward across the desk and asked, "How much do you know about Naomi Atossa?"

"Next to nothing. I deplore the Madrian tendency not be open about the women of their society.

"When exactly did Eddan el Halugh die?"

"According to the Coroner, it was mid-week, around the ninth of this month. Why?"

"Naomi Atossa left Madras on the eight day of this month. And as far as I know she has no knowledge about Eddan el Halugh's death."

"She left for . . . ?"

Montoya only hesitated a moment. "Novalis. Members of her family came and took her back home. Since I am familiar with the Madrian reticence, I doubt you know the particulars about the marriage between Naomi Atossa and Eddan el Halugh."

Bakkar looked puzzled. "Particulars?"

"There is quite a story. Abduction is a mild explanation. Naomi left a trail of evidence all along the route from Sarpedion to Madras. Her plight is well documented." Montoya looked candidly at Bakkar, then told him Naomi's story.

Bakkar was stunned and sat motionless for a few moments. "And she says she was drugged most of the time?"

"Yes. We have several depositions from passengers and the Captain of the ship, Dream Boat. When Miss Atossa left for Novalis, she left under her own name."

"She never considered herself married to Eddan el Halugh?"

"No. She was very adamant about that."

"Did Hadjar el Halugh know?"

"Yes. At their first meeting, Naomi immediately apprised him of the situation."

"I see." Bakkar settled back in his chair digesting these revelations.

After a while, Montoya continued, "So according to your evidence, Eddan el Halugh died a day after Naomi Atossa left for Novalis."

"Yes. There is evidence that he may have died of a food allergy. There was a suspicious additive in the mollusks, possibly as an aphrodisiac. None of the other people suffered any ill affects. It could have been murder, or simply an accident. We have no proof either way. I hope the el Halugh family will accept this verdict. The coroner would like to write this case off as death by misadventure and close it."

There was a knock at the door and Montoya's secretary came in. "Sorry to interrupt, but you asked me to remind you about the meeting. It is in ten minutes."

Montoya rose, indicating that the interview was at an end.

Bakkar also rose. "Thank you for the information," he said with a slight bow and left.

* * * *

Saada was in her office going over bills with Boufaric, when Hadjar stormed in. "They closed the case!" he bellowed incensed. "No evidence of foul play," he continued, his rage mounting. "Inspector Bakkar says that Naomi has gone back to Novalis. He had the affront to tell me that according to other people's testimony, Eddan was never married to Naomi. What balderdash!" Hadjar's voice was a roar in the closed office. "She was pregnant, wasn't she? She slept with him!" There was black anger in his eyes as his fist came down on Saada's desk.

Hadjar was formidable and totally beyond reason in his rages.

When Saada looked at his face, she saw the unmistakable harshness. She had been married to him long enough, not to know this look. She had seen him carry on too many quarrels and controversies that began over small things, then, escalated into bitter, uncompromising feuds. He would be impervious to any arguments.

He turned on Saada. "You watched her closely. How did she get away, huh? Tell me that!"

Saada lowered her eyes. "I'm sorry, Hadjar," she said meekly.

"And you!" turning to Boufaric, "You wouldn't know, either! None of you mealy mouthed people know anything." He raised his fist and went toward Saada. For an instant, Saada and Boufaric both froze. Then Boufaric moved in to protect his mother.

Hadjar's eyes widened. Boufaric was taller and heavier, and Hadjar knew that Mustafa had schooled Boufaric in martial arts, as well. He recognized in his son a formidable opponent.

"Hadjar," Saada said quietly, "she's gone. There is nothing we can do about it. Her people came to get her. As Inspector Bakkar said, she must have planned on her escape since Sarpedion. She left a trail for them to follow." Saada sat perfectly still, frightened as Hadjar's face tightened.

"She, or her people killed Eddan, and they won't get away with it." The blood in his face darkened as he glared first a Saada and then at Boufaric.

"But, Father, she was gone . . ."

Hadjar broke in with a sarcastic tone. "Are you on her side now? She's carrying Eddan's child, and I want it back." He turned and stomped out of the room, slamming the door.

There was stunned silence.

"Mother?" Boufaric said.

"Don't, my son, don't. It's no good arguing with him when he's worked himself into this stage of rage."

"There are facts, and facts are sometimes inconvenient things. But as Bakkar said, Naomi was off Madras before Eddan was dead."

"I know. But right now your father won't accept the facts or any other possibilities."

"What are you going to do?"

"I'm going to wait."

* * * *

That night, Saada was long in falling asleep. Unable to lie still, she tossed and turned, her mind working at one plan, then another. Had Hadjar picked up on her insinuations? Maybe I could get him to pursue Naomi. I need something that will get him away from Oran. Even off Madras. Maybe there's a way to dry up his access to money. Leave him stranded on Novalis. At least for a while . . . maybe forever.

A few moments later she rose and putting on her qamis slipped downstairs and out into the garden. Her restless mind churned in furious turmoil. She walked outdoors until the chill of the night and her own physical and mental fatigue finally drove her back inside. As she went up, the stair creaked. She was about to reenter her room, when a sharp voice whispered, "Who is it?"

"I'm sorry Mari, it's only me," Saada replied quietly.

"Can't you sleep?"

"No."

"Where is all this getting us to?" Mari whispered. She had lived in terror ever since coming to Oran. As an orphan she had been foisted on unwilling distant relations. When Saada came to lay a proposal down from Hadjar el Halugh, the only decent thing her relatives did for her was to insist she have the status of a wife.

"We'll see. Don't be worried. Somehow, it will all work out."

It's easy for her to say, don't worry. How long will this continue? Lately, she was becoming unnerved by Hadjar's sudden appearances from behind. When he looked at her with his cold piercing eyes, she quaked. She was convinced his eyes could see through her, as if he knew she was hiding something. It had taken all her courage not to blab everything. "How long Saada, how long?" Mari whispered, anxiously.

Saada patted Mari on the arm and told her, "Until he makes up his mind about what to do."

Mari exhaled a long-held breath in a long sigh and with a slightly more hopeful note in her voice, she asked, "You will help it along?"

"We'll see. Go to bed, Mari. Morning will come soon enough."

"Good night, Saada. I hope you can sleep."

* * * *

Morning came quicker than anyone liked. When Hadjar came down to breakfast, he glowered at everyone. If by chance he overheard anyone mentioning Naomi's or Eddan's name, his face would harden into cold stone.

Mari tried to serve his breakfast as unobtrusively as possible.

Halfway through the meal, Hadjar's fists came down on the table. "She's not going to get away with it," he shouted, aimed at no one in particular. Hadjar had always been quick to become angry, and they all knew he bore long grudges. Everyone at the table flinched. As always, they took their cue from Saada.

She sat silently at the table with her eyes cast down, not speaking.

"By all the gods, I'm going to Novalis. I'll show her! Saada pack my clothes! I'm going to town."

With this pronouncement, he stormed out of the house. As the front door slammed shut, Saada lifted her eyes and gave a long sigh. It had worked. In his anger he was beyond reasoning and had succumbed to her subtle hints.

"Mari, help me pack." Saada looked at the three consorts, "Clean up the kitchen and do as much in the house as you can. Boufaric, go about your business."

Later, when Saada took a walk in the garden, Mari joined her.

"What are we going to do now?" she asked, troubled.

"We wait and see, and say nothing," Saada told her.

When Hadjar, still storming around like thunder, came back late in the afternoon, he went to Saada's office. "I have taken out all our personal savings, except the money to operate Oran, I'm going to stay in Sikar. I have contacted the Embassy and requested a visa to Novalis. There's a ship leaving in three weeks. Where's Boufaric?"

"Moshja knows."

Chapter Fourteen

Mariam was standing at her living room window watching Naomi as she ambled down the road toward the Nunnery. Naomi's gait was slow and ponderous.

She's not the same, Mariam thought sadly. Not since Caleb died and now all this. I want my sunny, carefree girl, laughing and singing, and full of mischief back. No, but this Naomi is quieter, more introverted. Then Mariam thought about the baby. Maybe the baby will make a difference, she hoped and then smiled.

Coming into the room, Naomi was slightly out of breath from climbing up the flight of stairs. "Hello, Aunt Mariam."

"You look hot. Come sit down on the couch and put your feet up." Once she was situated, Mariam put a pillow behind her back and another one under her feet.

Naomi leaned forward and kissed her aunt on the cheek, "Quit fussing over me; I'm fine."

"Would you like tea?"

"Something cold would be better. I don't know . . . I'm getting so big and clumsy. I will be glad when all this is over," she said dolefully.

"It won't be much longer," Mariam consoled her, "How about some iced peppermint tea?"

"That sounds good."

Mariam picked up the house phone, "Two glasses of iced peppermint tea, please."

Naomi had to smile. "What's new?"

"We are still trying to get all the vouchers gathered so we can pay the debts you've incurred," Mariam grinned.

It was said in jest, but Naomi flushed. "I'm so sorry . . ."

"I'm not," Mariam interrupted firmly.

The door opened and Hanna, the Nunnery's housekeeper, came in. As far back as Naomi could remember, Hanna had been part of the family. Hanna had taken a great liking to the then lively and at times mischievous little girl when she came home for vacation. She now smiled at Naomi, her eyes crinkling. "How are you child? Poor thing, you look all hot and give out. You shouldn't have walked all the way out here in your condition," she chided her.

"Hello, Hanna. I'm fine, but thirsty. How have you been?"

"Oh same as always. Just a little slower. Are you going to stay for supper?"

Naomi looked at Mariam.

"Yes, she's staying for supper. Either way, Sarah wants to see her."

"All right. All it will take is another plate."

After the door closed behind Hanna, Naomi asked, "How is Grandmother taking all this; I mean the debt?"

"Your Grandmother is happy to have you home. Anyway, most of it will be paid by the el Halugh family."

"I wish I could be rid of that memory. They were dreadful people," Naomi whispered, making a grimace, her lips pulled thin. The memory of Eddan and his face filled her thoughts, overwhelming her with a powerful loathing. Naomi looked past Mariam, recalling the degradation and rape. She shook her head and with effort continued. "The time I was with Eddan, I was always frightened. I began to be afraid of him soon after we were on that ship and didn't know why. When I met him, he seemed so polite and good tempered. Then one day I realized that it had all been an act, a role he played. Living on Eubea, I was always sick with fear. There were days I thought I couldn't bear it any longer."

Mariam reach for Naomi and pulled her into her arms. "My poor love, I wish I could wipe those memories away. Some day, they will be in the past, just as now, you have a future. Just think you will have a child to care for."

"Thank God, it isn't Eddan's. I'm not sure if I could love it if it were his."

Taking Naomi's face between her hands, Mariam looked into her saddened grey eyes and wondered where all the mischievous sparkle had gone. "It is your child, Naomi," Mariam told her firmly.

"I'll try to think of it as mine." Then, with obvious aversion, she asked, "I won't have to see them again?"

"No, the Embassy lawyers and your father will handle it. Jarrod is the litigant in this case, accusing the el Halugh family of kidnapping you. All he needed was your affidavit and the deposition from the other people. You created enough of a paper trail."

"Thank God. I couldn't face seeing any of them." She looked down at herself and gave a deep sigh as she patted her belly. "I just hope this won't take much longer."

"Grandmother assures that it's not going to be much longer."

Suddenly, Naomi chuckled. "It's funny having a Grandmother who is a midwife. I hope she's right, because I'm getting so uncomfortable."

"I don't know about being pregnant, but looking at you, I can understand."

For a long time they sat silently sipping the tea, busy with their own thoughts. Suddenly Naomi spoke. "I know I'm home and free again, but I still feel like I'm dreaming. I am still working on piecing it all together . . . how all this was arranged."

"Very indirectly. The only one we know for sure who helped was Sidi el Asnam."

"Yes, he told me that in all good conscience he could not have an offspring of his grow up in the el Halugh family. That was what prompted him to help me."

"You were never without friends, remember that." After a while Mariam asked, "Are you staying overnight?"

"No, I still need to study. My bar exam is tomorrow. I just couldn't stay cooped up in my room any longer, so I came out here."

"You know, your father would like for you to move in with him."

"I know. I told him I would think about it."

"Fair enough. I'll have someone drive you home after supper. Grandmother should be here shortly. She wants you to fill out some legal papers about the baby."

* * * *

Two years had passed, and Jarrod sat in the chair behind his desk, surveying his office with great satisfaction. Everything was new and elegant, yet not ostentatious. He was at the start of his career as a private lawyer. Currently, he only had a few clients, but he was confident that in due time this would remedy itself. His staff consisted of Naomi, who was now his junior partner, a young male paralegal and a middle-aged secretary. He had a spacious apartment in the five-story building owned by the Darbani family. It was very conveniently located on the second floor just above his office.

After their graduation from law school, the office and the apartment both would have been Naomi and Caleb's place. Then there was the car accident that killed Caleb. A year later, the Embassy had assigned him to Sarpedion. Looking back, it seemed a hundred years ago. Before moving in, he had checked with Naomi to be sure it would not bother her in any way, and she had smiled and reminded him that she had never lived there. So why would I mind? she had added.

A week before the opening of the office, he had finally persuaded Naomi to move in with him, pointing out that the apartment was considerably large just for him. His persuasion had included how much easier it would be on her and two-year-old Calita. You won't have to drive in all the way from the Nunnery, he added.

Calita, Naomi's daughter was now almost two years old.

Jarrod had just picked up a document when his secretary knocked and opened the door. There was a broad grin on her face. "Mister Darbani, I think we have our first important client."

"Well, don't just stand there. Who is it?"

He rose from his seat as his secretary opened the door wider and Sarah Atossa sailed in. She stopped in front of his desk.

"Hi, Jarrod," she said briskly, "Are you open for business?" Jarrod's mouth quirked into a smile as he looked at her. He liked her a lot. She reminded him of Lia, or was it Mariam?

"What a question, Sarah? Of course I'm open for business.

Would you like to take a seat?" he asked, pointing to the chair at the front of his desk.

"No, thank you. I'll be just a minute. I'm in town to see about the auction."

"Then, how can I be of assistance?"

"You already know that old Levi died. I decided to put the legal affairs of the Nunnery into your hands, since you're already handling the vouchers coming in from Naomi's debacle. So, tomorrow, expect the transfer of our records to your office."

"Thank you, Sarah. I will take care of it."

She smiled at him and turned to leave.

"Sarah, wait! I almost forgot. Naomi asked me to tell you she will be coming out to your place after she picks Calita up from daycare."

"Will you be coming, too?"

"Not today. Tell Mariam I have papers for her to sign and would like her to plan on having supper with me."

"I will tell her. You are coming to my auction next week?"

"Wouldn't miss it, but do you really want to sell off all the wine?"

"It's one way of paying Naomi's debts. Are you aware that the el Halugh family didn't pay nearly enough to cover one-third of the expenses we incurred. I wanted to launch a protest, but Naomi said I shouldn't."

"Sarah, you must understand. Good, bad, or indifferent, Naomi is trying to put this whole ordeal behind her. She wants no contact whatsoever with the el Halugh family. Especially now since she has Calita to consider. You probably are aware she still has nightmares? It must have been hell for her."

"I know, poor girl. I heard her screaming one night when she was at the Nunnery. This is the only reason I'm agreeing to drop this whole affair. Selling the wine, plus the money you provided, will help. Did you know that the wine was cellared fifty years ago? One of the best years we had."

With a twinkle in his eyes, Jarrod said, "I had hoped to drink at least part of it."

She smiled with some internal amusement, and he suddenly felt annoyed.

"You and Mariam?" she asked with a slight lilt in her voice.

"As soon as this mess is over."

"I'll keep at least one bottle."

"I wonder what Naomi will say?"

"Probably congratulate the both of you. Well, I need to go and I'll give Mariam your message."

* * * *

Naomi decided it was too late to take Calita to the Nunnery, so she left her with a baby sitter. She was only going to be gone for a little while. The last of the vouchers had come in that afternoon, and after Naomi figured the total, she was shocked. It was prohibitive. The vouchers covered Jarrod and Mariam's travel from Novalis to Sarpedion and then from Madras back to Novalis. Only the travel from Sarpedion to Madras was covered by the Planetary Alliance's legal department, since that trip had been in pursuit of a felon.

The day was marvelous, a bright blue sky full of sun and a few wispy clouds. Naomi drove leisurely toward the Nunnery, listening to her favorite music. She felt a little guilty that her grandmother was going to auction off the vintage wine she had hoarded and cherished in the deep cellars of the Nunnery. A bottle was brought up only on very special occasions.

She was just entering the long curved driveway when a speeding car came barreling down the road heading toward her. It sideswiped Naomi's car, driving her off the road. For a harrowing second she though she'd seen the angry face of Hadjar el Halugh. It took every bit of her driving skill to get the car under control and to head straight on the road again. Stark fear was etched on her face as she floored the accelerator and sped toward the house. She slammed the gear into park and tumbled from the car. Scrambling to her feet, she raced toward the front door. Once in the foyer, acrid fumes assaulted her nose, all but knocking her out. She removed her blouse and pressed it against her face, but it was no barrier for the stinging odor or the burning sensation in her throat and nasal passages. She quickly turned and went back outside and around the house. Picking up a shovel left in the flower bed, she broke out a panel in the patio door. Wrapping the blouse around her hand, she reached through the broken glass, and opened the door. Suddenly, her eyes and skin began to burn and she was blinded. Groping along the outside wall, she smashed one window after the other. During all her efforts, she was aware of distant sirens.

Someone suddenly grabbed her by the shoulder. A man's voice said, "Miss Atossa? I'm from the police. Please let me help you." He took her aside and laid her on the grass. Then someone poured a watery solution over her face and body.

"The paramedics are here," a woman's voice assured her.

"What happened?" Naomi asked, still unable to see.

"We don't know yet. We have people coming to help."

"My family?"

"There are people inside the house?"

"Yes. At least eight, plus the servants."

"We found the servants. They are all right. Most were in the basement-floor kitchen preparing the meal. And we found a woman, Sarah Atossa. She's the one who gave the alarm that brought us here."

"My grandmother? Where is she?"

"She's been taken care of by the medics. We also caught the perpetrator. Do you know a Hadjar el Halugh?"

"Oh god, oh god, oh god," Naomi moaned, turning on her side, she curled up tightly and passed out.

* * * *

Jarrod was just saying goodnight to Mariam when her phone began to ring. "I wonder who that is," she mumbled as she unlocked her door. "Come on in," she said over her shoulder to Jarrod. As she went to grab the phone, he sat down prepared to wait.

"There has been a what?" she suddenly shouted into the phone. "Oh my God which hospital? I'll be right there."

Hearing the dread in her voice, Jarrod had already leapt from his chair. Grabbing Mariam by the arm, he propelled her toward the door. "What happened?" he demanded.

"Naomi and my mother are at Central Hospital."

"What happened?"

"They wouldn't tell me."

At the hospital, they immediately rushed to the emergency room. The moment they came through the automatic doors, a policeman approached them.

"Jarrod Darbani?"

"Yes."

"I'm police commissioner Rabat . . ."

"Yes, I know," Jarrod interrupted him. "I'm here to find out about my daughter and mother-in-law."

"You have not been to the Nunnery?"

"No, Mariam Atossa received a phone call telling her that her mother and her niece, my daughter, are at this hospital."

"Mister Darbani, there has been an attack at the Nunnery. Except for your daughter and mother-in-law, and the servants, all are death."

Jarrod turned ashen and Mariam fell back a step and tried to speak but no sound would come. She went so pale Commissioner Rabat prepared for her to faint.

"Dead?" Jarrod echoed. Then visibly pulling himself together, he demanded, "What are you talking about? What kind of attack?"

"Poisoned gas. Does the name Hadjar el Halugh mean anything to you?"

Jarrod stared at him, and Mariam swayed on her feet, clutching at his arm.

Jarrod's voice reflected the panic soaring in his brain. His "Yes," was barely audible.

Mariam shuddered at hearing the name. She closed her eyes, and with her hands over her face, she could barely whisper. She said, "I think we need to hear the whole story."

"We received an emergency call from Sarah Atossa. She said she needed medics and police to come out to her place. She described the car and gave us its tag number. There was a police cruiser in the vicinity and it was immediately diverted to the Nunnery. It was in time to intercept the car speeding away. The driver was immediately arrested. In the meantime, the medics arrived and were directed to the house. They found a Naomi Atossa trying to open windows and doors. She had apparently been inside, but had the presence of mind to immediately back out. Inside we found eight people, three of them children, killed by a poisoned gas. Your mother-in-law, Sarah Atossa, had been in the cellar. She was only slightly affected by the gas. I have already tried to interrogate Hadjar el Halugh, but he is very uncooperative. When we asked him if he wanted his embassy notified, he declined. Now, can you tell me of any motive for someone to attack your family?"

"Commissioner Rabat, after I've seen my mother and niece, we both need to speak to Hadjar el Halugh," Mariam said. "It will be the easiest way to get to the facts."

"I will be here waiting for you."

"Thank you, Commissioner," Jarrod told him. He turned around to face a doctor coming toward them.

"Are you relatives of Sarah and Naomi Atossa?"

"I'm Naomi's father and this is Sarah Atossa's daughter. How are they?"

"The older lady is fine, albeit shaken. She has inhaled very little of the gas which has only slightly affected her lungs and eyesight. The younger woman is in an oxygen tent. She should be all right, but we are also concerned with her reaction. She is in fetal position and unresponsive."

Chapter Fifteen

"Oh, Lord," Jarrod said. "Can I see her?"

The doctor turned toward a nurse and instructed her to take Mariam to see her mother, while he took Jarrod to Naomi's room. When Jarrod entered the room, Naomi was curled up under the oxygen tent, attached to an intravenous drip. Both her eyes were bandaged.

Jarrod looked down at his daughter and his eyes filled with tears. Carefully, he pushed the plastic sheet of the oxygen tent back and sat down on her bed. Stroking her hair away from her face, he whispered her name and got no reaction. He felt a great heaviness. Disheartened, he took her hand and began massaging it gently.

"Jarrod." Sarah's voice said softly behind him.

He turned to see that Mariam had wheeled Sarah into the room. She looked pale and hunched in the chair.

"She's not responding. She just lies there," Jarrod said, despairingly.

"Mariam, push me up to the bed," Sarah told her daughter.

Sarah took Naomi's hand and patted it lightly. "Naomi, it's time to come around," she told her granddaughter peremptorily.

"Mom, she won't. It's too much for her to face right now."

Sarah sat quietly for a moment, thinking. "Where's Calita?"

"Still with her babysitter."

"Call and tell her to bring Calita here. If Naomi responds to anything, it will be to Calita's voice."

"While you're waiting for Calita, I will go with the Commissioner to see Hadjar el Halugh."

Puzzled, Sarah asked, "el Halugh? He did this? But why?"

"Revenge most likely. But I would like to find out why, too."

"But this is ludicrous," Sarah said.

"To any normal person, yes, but not to the person Naomi's described to us." Mariam shrugged and raised her hands in a helpless gesture.

Not long after Mariam had gone, the babysitter arrived, carrying Calita.

"Hi, Sweetie," Sarah said gently and motioned for Jarrod to bring the little girl close to the bed.

"Hi, Grandy," Calita said. Then pointing to the bed, there was a small, concerned catch in her voice. "My Mommy?" she asked.

"Yes Calita. Come, wake Mommy up," Sarah told her.

Jarrod pushed the plastic aside and set her on the bed. "Talk to Mommy, Calita."

Calita tugged at Naomi's arm. "Mommy, wake up. Wake up Mommy!" When Naomi didn't respond, Calita grew frightened and shook her arm. "Mommy, wake up!" she demanded. "Mommy! Calita wants you. Mommy!"

There was a mumble from Naomi and then her hand, fumbling, reached out to touch her daughter. "Calita?"

"Naomi, this is your Grandmother. Do you know where you are?"

"I can't see!" came her alarmed reply.

"Because your eyes are bandaged, love."

"Why?" Then after a while, "What happened?"

"You don't remember?"

There was a hesitant, "No."

"You went to the Nunnery," Sarah prompted.

"A car ran me off the road," she replied, incensed at the recall. Then, after a pause, she asked, "Hadjar? I saw him. I'm sure I saw him. What did he want at the Nunnery? Grandmother!"

"Don't worry about him. The police have him locked up."

Naomi let go of her daughter and tried to touch her other arm. Jarrod caught it to prevent her from dislodging the IV.

"Did I get hurt in the car?"

"No, Naomi," Jarrod told her.

"Father?"

"Yes, I'm here, too."

Naomi furrowed her brow, and instantly remembered. "My eyes and my skin were burning."

"The doctor has taken care of that," Sarah told her.

"Yes, but . . . I tried to open all the windows and doors. Someone grabbed me . . ." Then a sharp and loud cry, "What happened at the Nunnery? Hadjar. What did he do? Why did my eyes and skin burn?"

"It was poisonous gas," Sarah told her.

"Poisonous gas? Oh, no. Grandmother, who was in the house?"

"Your cousins."

"The babies?"

"They, too."

"Oh, Lord. God!" Naomi wailed and began to tear at the bandages. She arched her body and began to make inarticulate sounds.

"Naomi, stop it!" Sarah said sternly, "You're frightening Calita."

Naomi subsided. "When will this nightmare end?" She spoke angrily, balling her fists.

Sarah noted the anger and was glad for it.

"I need to get out of here," Naomi suddenly cried.

"As soon as the doctor releases you," her father told her.

"Calita?"

"I'll take care of her. I think Mariam and I can manage looking after one little girl, right Calita?"

Naomi was kept for a week in the hospital for observations. Mariam came as often as she could, bringing Calita to see her mother.

* * * *

Naomi was only three days home from the hospital, and despite her father's protestation, insisted that she be allowed to work. Though it didn't include sitting in court with him, at least he was allowing her to do research for his cases.

A week later she had come home about mid-morning from the courthouse to find a note propped up on the kitchen table. It was from her father requesting a meeting with her at noon in the restaurant across from the courthouse.

Naomi pursed her lips. She had promised Calita a trip to her favorite toy store to buy a gift for her best friend's birthday. She would just have to bring her along and do the shopping later.

When Jarrod walked into the restaurant, Calita saw him first. She wriggled off her mother's lap and ran to meet him.

"I waiting for you," she told her grandfather.

"Thank you. That is very nice of you."

He swept her up into his arms, and Calita put both hands to his cheeks and gave him a resounding smack on the lips.

Jarrod chuckled and wagging her chin, asked, "Are you happy your Mommy is home?"

"Yes. Mommy feeled better."

"Hello, Naomi. Calita says you are feeling better."

"Yes, much better. Sorry, I had to bring her."

"That's no problem."

"Did you find out?"

"We need to talk."

Although his face was calm, she could sense uneasiness beneath the surface. When she looked up at him, his eyes turned bleak.

"Then you've spoken to Hadjar? Why did he do it?"

"He won't talk to anyone. He said he will only talk to you."

Naomi's mouth began to quiver. She swallowed several times before she finally whispered, "Father, I can't."

Jarrod felt his heart wrench. As he studied his daughter, he could well imagine the fear, or even terror it would arouse at seeing Hadjar el Halugh again.

"You might have to, Naomi," he told her gently.

"Let's eat first, then we can discuss what to do about Hadjar el Halugh," Mariam interjected quickly, having approached the table unnoticed.

Only after dinner, when they were lingering over a cup of coffee and Calita was busy with her ice cream, did Mariam again refer to the subject. "To put an end to this, Naomi, I think you will have to face Hadjar. We need to know why he did what he did. It was most likely something to do with revenge . . ."

Naomi gave a start. "Revenge! Revenge for what?" she exploded. "I haven't done anything to them except try to get away. Eddan is not with him, is he?"

"No. He never mentioned anything about Eddan."

"That's strange. He would be the only one to have a legal complaint according to Madrian law. I still don't get what happened. I think it's about time you two filled me in."

"I know," Jarrod said. "We were waiting for you to feel more like yourself."

"What made you go out to the Nunnery?" Mariam asked.

"That afternoon, the last bill came in and I added them up. I was going to give it all to Grandmother."

"Yes, and . . ." Jarrod wanted Naomi to rekindle her memory to work through the incident. Perhaps she will get to a point she will want to confront Hadjar without my pushing her, he thought.

"Oh, Father," Naomi said, and sighed. "Let's see. I was making my way up the drive, when a car came barreling toward me, forcing me off the road. I was busy trying to get the car back under control, and for a split second I thought I'd seen Hadjar's face. I sped up to the house and when I entered the foyer, my skin and eyes started to burn and I went nearly blind. I ran back outside and around the house. I think I knocked the glass out to open the patio door. I guess I tried to open the windows."

Yes, by knocking most of them out."

"I did? I don't remember. Now you tell me the rest."

"As far as we can figure, everyone except Sarah was in the family room watching a play. Hadjar must have entered the house and thrown a poisoned gas canister into the room, then left. Sarah said she heard the door open and then close and thought it was you. As she came up from the cellar and moved into the hallway, she saw someone sneaking out. She immediately went back down the steps, and looking through the cellar window, got a glimpse of the man and the car's tag number and called the police. Luckily, there was a patrol car in the vicinity. The police were alerted about a possible break in, so they came immediately. That's how Hadjar was so quickly apprehended. His trial will start next week. The presiding judge has cleared his docket to expedite the matter. So to find out why, you will have to speak to Hadjar."

Naomi's face clouded. In a half whisper, she managed to say, "Mariam, those were dreadful people."

* * * *

It took Naomi the better part of a week to get her courage up to face Hadjar el Halugh. She dressed carefully that morning, drove herself there and parked the car. She took her attaché case along as she walked up to the prison gate.

At the gate she was met by a guard who had watched her approach. To his, "What can I do for you?" she handed him the visitor's pass she had previously obtained.

"Ah, a lawyer to see our alien from Madras." he said genially.

The gate opened and she was allowed inside.

"Go up to the white building where you will be met by a guard who will escort you to the cellblock."

Inside the white building, Naomi was reminded of a police station. She approached the counter and spoke to an officer. "I am Naomi Atossa, here to see Hadjar el Halugh."

"We have been expecting you, Miss Atossa." The guard turned toward a back room and called, "Hey Jake, come and escort Miss Atossa to cellblock five."

They walked the short path to a single-storied, red brick building in silence. Naomi was glad of it. She was shivering and her legs were growing unsteady. Inside, a female guard checked her identification, then asked her to open her briefcase and gave it a cursory look. Then she was respectfully frisked. There was a brief smile when the guard's hands came to her shaking knees. "Please come with me," she said.

A tight knot formed in Naomi's stomach as she followed a second guard along a narrow corridor to an iron gate. Someone had either pushed a button or pulled a lever. There was a humming noise and the steel door slid open and closed, then clanked to lock behind her. Once through the door, she was picked up by another guard. It was a long corridor to the interrogating room and she was tempted to turn back around and flee.

A final guard was stationed in front of an unmarked door.

"Mister Halugh is already waiting," he told her. Before he opened the door, she put her hand against the wall and closed her eyes.

"Are you all right?"

She looked up at him. "Yes," she answered and after he opened the door, added, "Thank you." When she stepped into the room, she paused, and when the door clanked shut behind, she needed to lean against it.

Hadjar looked strained and tired. There were shadows around his eyes. He sat shackled to his chair. His face was drawn and he appeared to be much diminished. He smirked when he looked up and saw her face.

"I apologize for not rising to greet you."

Naomi stood still and stared. His voice seemed to come from a long way off. It was with great effort that she focused on him and all her willpower to meet his eyes. Then a feeling of revulsion started, cold and stark, giving her the courage to face him. She stepped up to the table and gently placed the briefcase on top. Clearing her throat and hoping her voice wouldn't shake, she asked, "You wanted to talk to me?" as she took out a recorder.

"Why are you recording this?" he asked.

"So there is no misunderstanding," she answered clearly and pushed the play button. Naomi gave the place and date of the interview, then said. "Now, what do you have to say to me?"

He glared at her. "You have not asked about your husband," he said icily.

"Hadjar el Halugh, I have no husband . . ."

"Because he's dead," Hadjar flung at her.

Naomi gaped momentarily, then, swallowed hard. She had discomfited him with her look of disbelief. "He's dead?"

"You didn't know?" Hadjar asked his voice still harsh.

Naomi took a deep breath and closed her eyes. "No, I didn't know," she said, huskily.

"Why did you have him killed?"

"Killed?" she echoed and stared at him. "He is dead?" Naomi was almost sick with relief when the fact finally penetrated.

"The police found him. He had been dead for three days."

"Found him, where?"

"In Sikar . . . in the apartment he had rented."

"What apartment? How did he die?"

Hadjar was furious. A blind, incensed rage boiled inside him as he glared at Naomi sitting there motionless. A monstrous thought rose in him. Saada!

"How did he die?" Naomi asked again.

"He was poisoned," Hadjar said in a dull voice."

"When?"

"The last time anyone saw him, was the ninth of Adar, and he was found dead three days later."

"By then, I was gone from Madras. I left on the eighth, Hadjar. No one of my family killed Eddan. We had no reason to kill him. I was free and I was going home. In time, I would have had the so-called marriage annulled. My father had enough evidence. Now, why did you come all the way to Novalis?"

"For the child." It was the last ace he had and he hurled it at her.

Naomi was exhaling slowly. Sentimentality was not one of Hadjar's virtues and rising in her was red hot anger. She remembered Hadjar's possessiveness that would not let her go. "No, Hadjar," she said as calmly as she could. "I don't think so. Tell me, why did you come to Novalis?"

Hadjar rubbed his forehead. Minutes passed. Neither looked at the other, while Hadjar sat brooding. Yes, why did I come, when I could have stayed at Oran, at home, instead of in this prison? His gaze was fixed on something on the floor. He avoided looking at Naomi when he said, "I was angry. I wanted to punish you. I thought you killed Eddan. And then there was this child. Eddan's child."

"Hadjar el Halugh. I did not give birth to Eddan el Halugh's child."

He came halfway out of his chair, "Why, you . . ."

"My child is not Eddan's," Naomi said again and quickly added, "He had another man have intercourse with me. It was intercourse and not rape. That's how I knew it wasn't Eddan. And I was drugged at the time."

"Who?" The question exploded from him.

Naomi flinched. To protect Sidi el Asnam, she had to be convincing. She made an effort to quell the rising fear inside. "I don't know, Hadjar," she said as calmly as she could and met his eyes.

His face tightened and his hands clenched tightly above the table. "Why would Eddan . . ."

"Eddan could not have children. He was sterile."

Hadjar glared at her as if she had struck him, anger flooding his face. It was savage and violent. "What are you saying? He was my son. You're lying." The rejoinder came rapidly, hissing through his teeth.

Naomi bit her lip; she felt a slight pity for him. "No, Hadjar, it is true. He was afraid you would kill him if you found out."

There was a sudden and sickening return of memory. Eddan, an illness, the doctor's warning him about sterility. He hadn't wanted to hear about it. He had forgotten about it. He still didn't want to think about it.

"How did you get off Madras?"

"My father came and took me home."

"Your father?" Hadjar's voice rose harshly in disbelief. "He just came and took you home?"

"Hadjar el Halugh, I had been in contact with the Novalis embassies on Sarpedion and on Madras. My father was at all times informed of my whereabouts. He came and rescued me."

"But, then who killed Eddan?" he asked.

Naomi took a deep breath. "Hadjar, I don't know who killed Eddan," Naomi said, impatiently. "I didn't even know where he was. He had been gone from Oran for several weeks. What killed him?"

"They said something in his food."

"His food? Did he eat oysters?"

Hadjar banged the table with both fists, "He couldn't eat oysters. He was allergic to them," Hadjar shouted angrily.

Naomi gave him a long look. "Yes, he did. He used them as an aphrodisiac. He believed they heightened his potency. But it made him crazy. Every time he ate oysters, he raped me," she shouted. Then, somewhat calmer, she told him, "Hadjar, no one killed Eddan. He probably died from an allergic reaction to the oysters he'd been eating. Didn't the doctors tell you that?"

Hadjar brought both his arms with the chain down on the table, and then rose as if he would fling himself at Naomi. The guards immediately rushed into the room, restraining him.

Naomi rose. She was tired. This interview had taken longer than she'd wanted and had taken more out of her than she'd thought. With deliberate care, she turned the recorder off, and placed it back into her attaché case. She then looked at the man who had caused so much havoc to her family.

"Hadjar, there was nothing to avenge. What you did, was all for nothing," Naomi spoke in distinct, individual words. "Hadjar, you're a fool. You have always been a fool. You are a very stupid man."

His face visibly withered.

Naomi turned and left.

* * * *

When he was escorted back to his cell, Hadjar was numb. He sat on his bunk, his head between his hands, oblivious to everything.

It was all for nothing. Naomi's voice echoed in his head. Then he saw Saada's inscrutable face. Did she manipulate me? The many nights alone in his cell, he had agonized over it.

He had come back from Sikar that day and found his suitcases packed. Silently, she had accompanied him as he walked out of his house. She had shown no emotion, her face had been as unreadable as always. She never tried to stop him, even agreed with him that someone had murdered Eddan and with very subtle insinuations, she had pointed to Naomi.

He could see that now. Saada had fed his anger.

When his money had run out, he had tried to wire for more, but his accounts were closed. When he had written to Saada, his letters were unanswered. His last letter, telling her he was in prison and needed money to hire a lawyer, came back as undeliverable. In desperation, he wrote to Boufaric and later to Mustafa. No replies.

All the exaltation from having avenged Eddan slowly trickled away and left him empty and cold. He was caught and he had no defense.

He felt cheated. Even Naomi had cheated him. No grandchild. Hadjar rose and in defeat began beating his fists against the wall.

* * * *

The next day, the guard informed him his lawyer wanted to see him. "What for?" Hadjar asked.

"I don't know. You want to go or not?"

Hadjar knew there wasn't any hope, but it was better than sitting in his cell.

"I'll go," he told the guard.

When Hadjar stepped into the room, his lawyer was sitting on top of the table, lazily swinging his leg. He was young and fresh out of law school. Because Hadjar was an indigent, he was entitled to a public defender, and this new lawyer had been given the job, because no one else wanted it.

"What do you want?" Hadjar asked sullenly.

The lawyer looked at Hadjar. He instantly disliked the skinny, arrogant bastard as he dubbed him. "To close the case. There was never any chance for you; you knew that. I have some papers for you to sign."

"What for?"

"To let the State know to whom you want to leave your worldly possessions."

Hadjar sneered at him. "You can have whatever I've got. Maybe it will cover your fee."

"Fat chance," the lawyer told him. "Have you any family?"

"Apparently, not," Hadjar said, and signed the paper.

The lawyer, whose name Hadjar could never remember, shrugged. "That's it," he told him and placed the signed paper in his briefcase. He snapped the top shut, then, stood for a moment to look at his client. "Well, goodbye," he told Hadjar. Wishing him good luck would be a misplaced sentiment he felt, so he simply walked from the room.

There was an appeal, but because of the heinousness of the crime, it was denied.

* * * *

The hearings were over and there was no clemency. Hadjar lay in the darkness and watched the late news. He had eight hours to live.

His thoughts went back to his first wife. He had married her because he loved her and she had loved him. She had been strong-willed and proud. When his father had ordered him to kill their daughter, she had looked at Hadjar. He never forgot that look. She had despised him for not standing up to his father. He had never seen so much loathing and revulsion when her eyes first raked over her father-in-law and then him. She had taken her dead infant, walked out of the house and thrown herself over the cliff. He had never recovered from her death. He had become cold and cruel. His mind went to Eddan's mother, but skipped over her memory to Saada. Saada hated him. He knew that now. He should have listened. But he had always been loath to take anyone's advice.

He thought of Naomi. I should have let her go. All this misery for nothing. Slowly he began to accept that Eddan had died of an allergic reaction to the oysters. He had known of the allergy. All these people had died for nothing, and so would he.

The next morning, the physician came and Hadjar wondered, why bother? I am going to die, anyway. After the physical, he was led to a small, white-washed room to wait. There was a flimsy cot and he sat on it. He had refused the cleric's aide, thinking, I don't need a priest or whatever they call themselves. So he sat on the cot, alone.

Hadjar el Halugh had been duly convicted and executed. He died alone, far away from home for the massacre of Naomi's family.

* * * *

A year later, Naomi and Calita returned to the Nunnery. One of the servants told her that her grandmother was in her apartment. She went up the flight of stairs and knocked on the door.

A surprised, "Come in," echoed from within. "Naomi, since when do you knock," Sarah asked, when she stepped into the room.

"Since I'm coming as a supplicant," Naomi told her, trying to look humble.

Sarah laughed. "All right, what are you asking?"

Naomi looked at her solemnly. "Can Calita and I come to live at the Nunnery?"

Sarah gave a surprised look. She didn't realize it, but she was holding her breath as she asked, "You wish to live here?"

Naomi hadn't grown up there, because her mother had sworn never to set foot onto the estate again after Sarah had disagreed with her choice for a husband. Naomi had only come for summer holidays and then always alone.

"I think Calita needs to grow up in a place like this." With an impish grin, she asked her daughter, "We can't leave Grandy here all by herself, now can we, Calita?"

Calita, looking at her great-grandmother, nodded her head, "Mommy said you need someone to love you."

Sarah, her eyes tearing up, spread her arms, "Oh, Calita, I would love for you to give me a big hug and then tell your Mommy it would make me very happy for you two to come live with me."

"Are you certain it would make you happy if we come to live here with you?"

"Yes Naomi, it would. Because that is what the Nunnery has always been . . . a place to come home to."